Still Holding Hands

Ray and Hilda Beamer's Story of Love and Triumph over Alzheimer's Disease

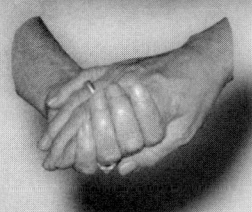

Stacie Ruth Stoelting; Age 15
— A Granddaughter's Portrayal —

Recommended and Endorsed by Randy Travis, Pat Robertson, and Senator Chuck Grassley

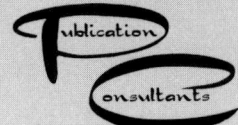

Publication Consultants

PO Box 221974 Anchorage, Alaska 99522-1974

ISBN 1-888125-88-8

Library of Congress Catalog Card Number: 2001097702

Copyright 2002 by Stacie Ruth Stoelting
—First Edition—

Notice of Clarification

Stacie Ruth Stoelting, of course, was not alive during all occurrences in her grandparents' lives (including their childhoods), consequently she was unable to include all of the firsthand details; some areas, therefore, have fictitious aspects. The events recorded, however, are elaborations from her grandparents' firsthand accounts and memories (according to their view points) as Stacie remembers and recorded them. As with any family, events are perceived differently by different members. Stacie recorded only her Grandma Hilda's and Papa Ray's personal reflections and recollections. This book is indeed accurate and true accordingly; conservatively stated, it is fiction based solely upon fact. Stacie's descriptions of Alzheimer's and related events are painfully, shockingly captured with all of its horrid realities.

All rights reserved, including the right of reproduction in any form, or by any mechanical or electronic means including photocopying or recording, or by any information storage or retrieval system, in whole or in part in any form, and in any case not without the written permission of the author and publisher.

Manufactured in the United States of America.

A HEARTFELT DEDICATION

Proverbs 16:3. "Commit your work to the Lord, and your plans will be established." This verse is a treasure to which I cling. It is an instrument by which I live. It is inspiring! Therefore, I begin my dedication with.......
I commit my book to the Lord!
Truly, I sincerely dedicate my book to my Best Friend: Jesus Christ, my Lord and my God! It is by Him I live and work. It is through Him that I attain my goals. I am **nothing** apart from Him. But.... With Him, I am something and with Him, this book will succeed. He has used so many people to bring this book to pass ....
He gave me my Papa Ray, my Grandma Hilda, and my Aunt Ruth; He helped me capture their lives. Grandma fears that the book may make her sound <u>too</u> <u>saintly</u>. (Well, to me, Grandma, you are a saint—a fun-loving one!) I dedicate it to them, the true heroes and fighters of the real battle with Alzheimer's. I admire and love them so much. (I have many stresses and insecurities like any teenager and they've always been there for me.)
He also gave me the privilege of having close grandparents on my father's side: Papa Otto and Grandma Alice. They have taught me priceless lessons (Which I've needed!), and which I'll not forget. Loving them, I also give them honor.
God placed me in a fantastic family; my parents are my fans and I'm a fan of them! They are incredible people

and oh, how I love them! (Attention to my sister Carrie Beth Stoelting—you're a super sister!)

My extended appreciation is directed to Dorothy and Lowell Perry for their interest and help in a beginning portion of my book's promotional tour. They are such special, dear people!

Jesus also bestowed upon me wonderful contacts: An influential, instrumental author deserves recognition: Mr. Glenn Guy (a.k.a. Dusty Sourdough). He is a talented, Alaskan author whose books I would recommend. (Thank you for encouraging me and contacting your publisher about me!)

It is with great appreciation that I express my gratitude to my publishing company and its leading consultant, Mr. Evan Swensen; without whom, I would still be a teenager in search of a publisher! He has been so wonderful! He's been patient, kind, and literally a God-send! (I guide people to read his works.)

And, with exceeding joy, I thank my incredible endorsees: Randy Travis, Senator Grassley, and Dr. Pat Robertson. They are remarkable people of character and honor. These people are role models for me. (I thank you all so much from the bottom of my heart!)

This dedication would not be complete without including all of my faithful friends and family whom I love and appreciate. They have been wonderful supporters of my book and my life; I thank God for all of them. I'm afraid that if I'd name them all, I'd forget someone! (Thank you, everybody!)

Now, I pray for you all:

"Dearest Father,

I pray for Your loving will to be carried out through my book and life to bless these people. Please, help them in some small way. Use my small book and me to glorify You. I'm so weak yet through You, I'll be strong. Help them to realize that, if You can use a "nameless" teen to write a book, You truly can do anything for anyone! Encourage my readers, Lord. Strengthen them through this. I ask that desires be fulfilled through this ministry which You've placed upon my heart. And, Jesus, I ask for a cure for Alzheimer's disease; I know that Your plan is best! Thank You, Lord, for all the wonderful surprises which You've brought and are bringing to my readers, my family and friends, and to me, too! You're wonderful, Lord! Thank You!"

In Jesus' name,
Amen.

TABLE OF CONTENTS

PROLOGUE

Before one can be fully sympathetic to other human beings' circumstances, the situations must be experienced. Whether a soul can fully comprehend the intricacies of human suffering or joy depends upon how much God has revealed to him. This book can never fully capture the bond of such a close, Christian couple as my grandparents, but maybe—just maybe—you can learn to become more sympathetic and even empathetic to the tragedy that millions face: Alzheimer's disease. This is Ray and Hilda's story...

Chapter One
"NO DAD! I CAN'T ..."

"Hello."

"Mama?" she calmly inquired. "How are things?"

"Do you really want to know?" she answered with her voice tired and sad.

"Was it a bad night?"

"Well, it could have been worse—he at least is settled in his chair watching TV-it's such a blessing, Mary."

"Did he wake you up a lot?" Mary inquired in genuine concern.

"We had a hard time getting him to bed...he talked so much you wouldn't believe it! All nonsense of course—something about different rivers and that he had to get to some meeting. We tried to coax him to go to bed—but it was no use. Ruth went to bed early because of her teaching job today so I tried to appease Ray. With this new medicine he seems to be so talkative. Anyway, I tried to get some sleep on the sofa. *The whole night, Mary, the whole night.*"

"Oh, Mama, I'm just so sorry. Daddy would never want you to go through this! He would say, 'Hilda, put me in a home!'," Mary pleaded.

"Oh, but Mary. Just yesterday he took my hand and said, 'You're my girl!' And we do have some good times .... He really enjoyed Ruth's dinner last night—she tried a new hot sauce and some Cajun rice. It was good," she said with admirable courage.

"But his care is so wearing, Mama, you've got to consider yourself! Many caregivers of those stricken with Alzheimer's are carried out before their loved ones!"

"I was at the doctor's and he didn't find any problem."

"Your blood pressure has skyrocketed."

"Well, it is so hard to let go.... We've had so many good times."

"Think of yourself."

"Oh, Mary! He's headed toward the bathroom. I've got to go. Send my love to all," Hilda said in sudden urgency staring as Ray strutted past her.

"We love you, too," Mary sadly though sincerely replied. How she wanted to some way reach through the telephone and help her! How she desired to some way reach her mother to make the decision to get assistance!

Hilda hung up the phone and rushed out of the kitchen as fast as an eighty-four year old could. She hurried as a mother would to help her child. But Ray was not her child; Ray was her husband.

"Come here, Ray," she said softly. She started to repeat the same instructions from a mere hour earlier. Gently, she attempted to explain where the bathroom was and how it was to be used.

"I've-got-to-pee," Ray managed to utter, slowly, with much difficulty.

"I know. You go in here," Hilda replied as she led her husband of fifty-six years into the bathroom.

— ❋ —

After Hilda had cleaned him up—the second pair of pajamas of the morning—she ushered him into the den. She helped him into his protected chair and briefly sat down on the covered sofa. Hilda placed her elbow on the armrest and rested her weary head on her hand. She tried to ignore the urine smell and Ruth's new plant that she hadn't wanted in the house. Hilda looked about the room. What had her dream home become? She could remember a time when the shelves weren't dusty and things were in their place. She could even remember how excited she had been when Ray and she had first seen the house. My! Had it been more than thirty years ago?

— ✻ —

Hilda and Ray Beamer, having just toured another house, walked down the sidewalk (side by side) to their car. Hilda had to look back at the white, four storied Victorian house once more to see it. Oh, how she adored this one! It was so stately…. and it had a porch! The kitchen was small-but Ray could fix that. The living room was so spacious. And a dining room—now she could have family over for holidays!

Ray helped Hilda into the car and she placed her gloved hands on her blue flowered special dress. She looked down as she smoothed her dress. Suddenly, she jerked her head up and smiled at Ray. He beamed.

"So, Hilda, did you like this last one?" he asked (knowing full well the answer)!

"Oh, Ray, it is wonderful! But how could we manage? The girls could have their own rooms, though. But it is expensive," Hilda was trying to spiral down to reality though her optimism kept her up and hopeful.

"Honey, with my new and better paying position at the school and if we would do without some luxuries, we just *might* be able to manage." Hilda in excitement kissed his cheek.

"But, you're right," Ray continued as he patted her hand. "The girls would enjoy different rooms!"

As he turned on the ignition, both smiled to think of how Mary and Ruth had used a rope to separate their room. There had been Mary's half and Ruth's half ….

By now they had pulled into the driveway of the house they had been renting. Before Ray could slam the car door, Ruthy ran up to the car with chestnut colored pigtails swaying. Her big blue eyes, sparkling with excitement, peered up into her father's loving face.

"Daddy, what was it like?" bubbled the little girl.

"Well, it ...."

"Did it have a porch?" the young voice interrupted.

"Yes, it had a porch," he tenderly replied stooping down to stroke his younger daughter on her head.

"Mama, was it pretty?"

"Oh, yes."

"Will you buy it?"

"We'll have to see." Hilda smiled and looked at Ray.

"I'll go get Mary! She'll be so happy!" Ruthy declared as she ran into the house slamming the screen door behind her.

"We didn't even give her a definite 'yes' and she's still excited! But do you know what? I'll give you a definite 'yes'," Ray beamed as he took Hilda's hand. Hilda gave him quite a kiss!

Into their now temporary residence they walked-hand in hand. Hilda had always thought that Ray had such well-shaped, artistic hands.

— ❋ —

"Hilda?!" Ray exclaimed with no warning, though with intensity.

"Yes, Ray," her sad voice replied.

The perplexity of his disease shone through his glazed-over expression. His fogged eyes gazed from beneath his furrowed brows. Delusions are as real to victims as the deep sadness loved ones feel because of them.

"Well! Why'd ... you ... leave me ... anyway?!"

"I haven't left you, honey; I'd never leave you. Now you just rest and maybe we could watch something on TV."

"Then, why didn't you go to my meetings? They're ... hard ..." his voice cracked in dreary frustration.

"You never told me about them."

"I should go there again, you know...." Muttering, he mellowed into slumber. His delusion was ceased only by merciful sleep. With the minor crisis settled, she began to tend to other necessary chores. After finding her way to the winding staircase, she prepared for her trek. Grasping the wide, oak banister she diligently proceeded. Her wedding ring made slight clinks against the wood doing so to the time of her steps. Clink ... clink ... clink ... clink; they ended when she finally faced the object of her ascension: their bedroom—now Ray's bedroom.

She yanked with all her strength the soaked quilt, the soaked sheets off the bed and then almost gave up on the mattress pad. It would be wet again in just a few hours anyway!

"How he manages this I'll never know," she whispered to herself as she gathered the bedding into her arms. Hilda hauled the daily load down the stairs again and plopped it into the washer. No sooner than the machine started, the phone rang.

She knew that she couldn't answer it before the second ring. She also knew Ray would be perturbed.

"Why can't you shut that thing up!!" Ray bellowed. Hilda, used to his radical behavior, ignored him and answered the phone.

"Hello," she said softly.

"Hi, Mom," Ruth said nervously. "I've had car trouble. After my morning class I was going to bring in lunch for all of us but my key wouldn't go into the ignition.

"What?"

"My key wouldn't go into the ignition.... It's weird. I'll explain when I get home. I'm sorry I can't be there for lunch. Are there any leftovers you two can eat?"

"We'll manage. Since you are only twenty minutes from home maybe Katy can pick you up."

"It's okay, Mom. Harry, the car guy, lives in town and he'll bring me home after work at about 4:00 PM." Ruth explained.

"Well, I'm sorry Ruth. Is Harry a nice, trustworthy man?"

"Oh, yeah, he has a nice car, too."

"How was your teaching job?"

"It was okay."

"Please, be careful, honey."

"I will, Mama," Ruth said softly.

As Hilda hung up the phone she said a quick prayer for her daughter. Her faith kept her going.

"Why, hello Cutie! How are you?" Hilda greeted as she stroked the obese tiger cat.

"My, you're getting fat—just like Dad Beamer's cat, Leon!" With just those few words, she immediately became immersed in memories of her long-dead father-in-law. He was dead, but alive in Heaven.... and in her memories.....

— ✸ —

Bernice Beamer loved to hold Leon on his lap. He would rock and Leon would sleep. No one touched Leon's vicinity. Leon loved Berny's lap. Bernice would stroke the robust cat with gentle, rhythmic steadiness. His large hand looked almost small in comparison with the huge cat!

Comparable to many, his cat brought out the softer side in him. He was not what you would call especially compassionate but he was an honest, God-fearing Presbyterian Christian. His personality possessed many aspects: He was strong; he was stern. He was kind; he was careful. He trustingly tried; he truthfully talked. Only when the conditions were right, he laughed. But when he laughed, he laughed hard! No one in the family could recount some of his storekeeper stories without laughing....

Berny, as a storekeeper, had experienced the unsolved puzzle: The (at times) unsolvable puzzle of dealing with people on a daily, one-to-one basis. Customers were friends and friends were customers. Without blinking an eye, a handshake would solidify an agreement. Rarely,

Berny would refuse a new charge account. Although such agreements sound ideal, they were not without their unforeseen difficulties.... such as with a certain lady....

For weeks, a woman (huge in stature) had frequented his business almost daily. Her figure, always draped in a dark dress, reminded many of a 50 pound flour bag tied tightly in the middle with a string. Always adorned with a fancy, flowered hat, she was easily located.

As she walked by many stores, storekeepers would release a slight sigh of relief when she waddled past their doors. With a hand always guarding her purse, she looked like a defensive guard dog. Her thin, gold, wire glasses (perched upon her pug-like nose) were round. Her small eyes—and even her large chin—were round! But, her personality was not well-rounded. She always exuded a sophisticated air and she never gave many compliments—though she voiced a host of complaints. Being a conscientious man, Berny had tried to win her over repeatedly. Day upon day, small talk would ensue; it was expected that it would entail entertaining entities of the day.

Berny was sweeping up in the back when he heard a familiar waddle; feet clogging down and approaching via the wooden sidewalk. He looked up with a startled countenance. A flowered hat jiggled by the lower portion of his store window—just beneath the painted letters. *She* had arrived.

The door was progressively pried open with her chubby, little hands, and she ushered herself into the store. With her nose pointed upward, with her fist shielding her precious handbag, she squinted up into Bernice's face. He, as always, not knowing what to say, began with the weather:

"Nice weather, isn't it?"

"Yes. There isn't a cloud in sight." Berny couldn't believe it! She actually was being optimistic. "But it'll probably storm by the end of week. It always does." (She always found the negative.)

"Well, I choose to hope it won't," Berny believed.

"You'll see. Something bad always follows the good. Just like floods follow rain, storms follow sunshine. The weather is disgusting to deal with. It even takes lives. Tornadoes tear through homes every year and kill people. Really, the world is tragic." With prolonged vowels, upon saying "the world is tragic," her expression appeared as a mourner's at a funeral. It made her face form a familiar, depressed, downcast frown.

She, still grimacing, hunched down near the lowest shelf. Sticking her nose as close to the butter without brushing it, she sniffed long and hard.

Straightening to her full five feet, she squinted into Berny's perplexed face:

"Is it fresh?" She scrunched up her nose in question.

No, I'm selling rancid butter," he thought, though did not say. Instead, he said: "Why, yes! It's quite fresh, indeed." He forced a smile—he had to keep his voice from sounding sing-song. All he wanted to do was tell her off!

"Oh, good.... That's a relief." She replied as she waddled over to the counter and placed a pound of butter down with a thump.

"Is this all for today?" Berny asked imparting her another smile that didn't come easily.

"Yes. But.... Mr. Beamer, where is that candy which you said would be arriving soon? You know that Johnny's birthday is approaching and I want to purchase a little bag." She raised her voice slightly in disgust. (She'd expected the candy immediately.)

"My, his birthday's comin' up that soon?"

"He'll be ten next week. But what about the candy?" She pointedly waved a finger as if she thought that it could cause the candy to appear.

"Well, it should be here by the end of the week. Tell Johnny to have a good birthday." Berny had to think of something to say so that he could "smooth it over."

"I'll tell him. But, it won't be the same without his favorite candy." She was going to persist at "harping" on her request. Yes, this type of customer is why many businessmen quit business. People, such as she, are the scratching on the chalkboard of enterprise.

"Well, thank you, Mr. Beamer." Berny thought he heard her whisper to herself: "*Well! It was the least he could do!*" But, Berny wasn't sure. At least, he hoped that he hadn't heard what he thought he'd heard. (He was becoming paranoid!)

With a fake, little smile, she parted with a bag under each of her strong, large arms. When he was sure that she was gone, he rolled his eyes.

Berny had tried his best to please her. Nothing he did ever could suffice. He knew that he'd be hearing about the candy for a very long time.

Yet, a different, more embarrassing problem haunted the back of his brain: No matter how hard he tried, his mind failed to remember her name! Even though she had established credit and was his least favorite customer, he couldn't remember that woman's name "for the life of him!" So, days passed and no clues were discovered....

Approximately one week following, Berny was whistling as he restocked the shelves. It was a great day. But, then, the sourpuss was back. His whistling adjourned upon the immediate approach of that familiar woman. The hat entered the store.

"Hello, Mr. Beamer."

"Hi." (Berny would never return her greeting with a name. He felt "hi" was safest.)

"How are you, Mr. Beamer?" She tried to impress him with cognate concern. It was futile. He saw beyond her fraudulent, smiling face.

"Yes, I'm doing just fine. And how's Johnny?"

"Oh, he's okay, considering. He was pleased with the candy—when he finally received it. It's his favorite, you know.... It's just too, too bad that it didn't arrive on schedule, Mr. Beamer." She would never allow him to dismiss his mistake.

Bernice and Nellie Beamer hold their firstborn—Alice. (Isn't she a beautiful baby?) Bernice and Nellie never dreamed of Ray at that time. However, within two years, he joined the scene!

"As I told you before, it was out of my control. I tried my best. The company was just running behind schedule, that's all." Once again, he tried to explain. But, this time her aggravating comments were not his source of agitation. She was due to pay her bills and he still couldn't recall her name! Oh, how he hoped that she'd give him a clue or something!

"Well, that will be all for today, Mr. Beamer. Which reminds me…. I need to settle my account."

"That's all right. I knew you'd take care of it one of these days." Berny felt himself take a strong gulp and a deep breath with a little nervous smirk crossing his face. He couldn't settle her account! He couldn't settle it without her name! He quickly thought of an excuse to buy him more time.

"All right. Let me get you an extra bag."

He bent down beneath the counter.... As he rustled and searched through the bags, a series of rushing last names flooded his head: "Woods, no, Wilson, no, Trimble, no, Coe, no, Carrington, no, Specht, no! Gee whiz! I can't think of it at 'tall!"

He knew that the community thought that he was an intelligent man. Oh, how he hated to ruin his reputation of being pretty sharp! It was such a small town, minor news traveled at the speed of light. He had to think of a "clever out" or else the gossiping ring of the town would hear of his mistake.

He thought: "Women would have a hearty laugh at me over many a' coffee.... They'd say, 'And to think that she'd come in for weeks and he still didn't know her name! *Didn't know her name! Didn't know her name!*' Then, those giggling ladies' laughter would ensue. Even my friends would have a good chuckle. And this time, I understand why! After all, I've seen and known this woman for weeks!"

"Ah, hah!" He said to himself. Suddenly, a clever thought crossed his mind. He popped up from behind the counter with a satisfied, smug smile.

"Could you tell me something?" He put on his most intelligent looking face as he pulled out his note pad and black, fountain pen. He got into his writing stance and leaned on the counter. "I want to make sure that I spell your name right."

(Good going, Berny.)

"How do you spell your last name?" With incredible self-satisfaction, with contented confidence, he smiled broadly—with an air of aptitude. But then.... His eyes practically popped out! He began to wonder what was wrong! All she did was stand there and stare with her big, round mouth open! It formed a gaping smile.... Then a loud laugh. Then a howl!

He blinked several times and tried to "kind of half-heartedly" laugh with her. After all, he hadn't done any-thing stupid, he was sure.

"You're really getting it now, Berny," he thought. He was puzzled and had a strange feeling wash over him.

In between her hearty laughter, her double chin became quadruple. Finally, she breathed out the spelling between chuckles: "Ha! Hoah! Ha! B-R-O-W-N! Brown, Mr. Beamer! Ha! Ha...."

Berny's skin turned pale........ Tears began to form.......... He braced himself against the wooden counter—he was laughing, too!

— ✳ —

That mere memory still seemed fairly real to Hilda. Though tragic, Hilda had difficulty recounting the good recollections of Ray's childhood and family—the disease had almost completely wiped away Ray's ability to relate any happy memories of his childhood.

The disease allowed Ray to disperse and reflect mostly upon his childhood's negative dimension. When well and balanced, Ray had been able to recount the joyful times with his sincere parents and special sisters.

The Bernice Beamer family would laugh together and enjoy singing. His sisters had come through for him various times throughout life.

(Now that they knew of his condition, they called often. They cared.) Both of his parents had been respected Sunday School teachers; they had been quite a couple—Nellie, with her strikingly expressive eyes, was quite pretty and Berny was tall and dignified.

Ray had been proud of his sisters' accomplishments; both of them had become terrific teachers. (All five of them: Berny, Nellie, Mildred, Alice, and Ray had been teachers! Some of his beloved nieces had carried on the strong family trait! Alice's beloved, devoted daughter, Dorothy, Mildred's exceptional Barbara, as well as Ray's Ruth Ann had all become teachers!) But, with the debilitating, desecrating disease, Ray had grown more and more pessimistic about his childhood and parents. Paranoia streaked his memories and mind like a dirty, clouded mirror. With the disease, he recounted his sad memories time upon time again.... Now, she, too, had begun to peer into the painful memories which he had repeatedly recounted within the beginning stage of Alzheimer's. The reflections of his clouded memory mirror took her to another time, another place....

— ❀ —

Yes, Berny was a complicated person. He loved to eat ice cream, to sell the Omaha Herald, and to discuss the Bible in detail. His fantastic voice blended beautifully as he was honored to be in a quartet. He always enjoyed singing the old songs. His eyes held a distinctive, special depth which few could describe. He was respected. He was Berny. Really, in later life, Ray looked like his father in that he was tall, thin, and had a receding hairline. To Ray, being a father meant being compassionate, loving, and always understanding. (It was little wonder that children loved Ray Beamer.) But to Berny, being a father to a son like Ray meant being a strict disciplinarian....

— ❀ —

Nineteen twenty-four. A year that Ray would not forget. A year in which a *certain incident* left Ray marred. He was merely eleven years old and the event was "to make a man out of him"—at least his father felt.

— ❀ —

The entire Beamer clan sat at the yellow clothed kitchen table; two sisters were his only siblings. Young Ray had somewhat contributed to the meal. He had picked some strawberries for his mother; he was certainly glad he had because she'd made jam!

He always enjoyed bread and butter but jam made it better! He had to have another slice. The jam was already within the grasp of his right hand. Ray's eyes scanned the table for more of Mom's homemade bread. He spotted it! It was just beyond his reach. But who would help him?

Alice sat across from him and looked especially happy. Then he remembered—she was trying out a new hairdo. Her black hair looked good before, Ray thought. But then again, she liked to look nice—she liked boys now. Mildred sat next to him. In a brother's eyes, she always seemed to be hard to please.

"Nothing I do seems to be good enough for *cute, little Mildred*. She'll probably discourage me from having a third slice. Just yesterday, she called me a pig just 'cause I'd eaten a couple of sugar cookies secretly. I didn't hurt anything. It even made me feel better after school; 'cause the kids teased me about my limp. Yup, I'd eat 'em all over again. Oh, of course, Mildred's sittin' next to Mom's right side. She always tries to be in 'her mama's good favor,'" Ray thought in a child's, in a sibling's spite. There was, sadly, some truth to his thoughts, however. Mildred didn't intend to hurt his feelings so much. She didn't realize that her comments cut him to the core. She had a good heart but (to Ray) a misguided mouth at times. (It was true especially when he teased her! And—being a big brother—teased her he did! Mildred had her side, too!)

Overall clad Dad sat across from melancholy Mom; Mom and Dad weren't speaking again. In fact, they hadn't been for two days. The fights when they raised their voices weren't as frequent now. Mother's big brown eyes glared across the table at Dad. Dad didn't seem to talk much. He just kept quiet. There were times that Ray even cried in fear that his parents would divorce. This child's fear had no means to be substantiated, but it was real to him. (As an adult, he was loved by children of damaged backgrounds. He could always relate to children with a similar fear.)

Ah, but he wouldn't let that bother him now! They could go ahead and stew! He wanted bread!

He looked at Alice. "She's the best chance I have," he thought. He stretched his leg and tapped her black, high laced shoe on the toe. She looked up and saw how Ray was gazing at the slices of bread. Slowly her petite hand pushed the blue plate piled with white bread in his direction. Cautiously, he picked up one of the thickest slices. Then the silence was broken. In brother Ray's, child eyes, Mildred was just "a little sister always after him." (One could readily see the brother/sisters relationship! Each one had thoughts and a side—similar to so many siblings!) To Ray's ears, Mildred's discouraging, correcting voice chimed:

"Oh, Ray! You've already had three pieces of bread. You don't want to get fat! Or do you?" She gave a concerned look which hid her underlying irritation. Her big brother always got the best bread pieces.

"Let the boy be, Mildred. After all, he is a growing boy," Dad defended. In fact, he gave a smile to Ray. At least it had been a smile until it reincarnated into a grimace when he turned to see Mom still glaring. Mom gave no word.

His parents didn't object after all! As he spread the gommy, thick jam onto his bread, he licked his mouth in anticipation. Grinning, he bit into it and savored the sweet preserves. Ray finished it and was ready to lick his strawberry adorned fingers; then he remembered he was at the table. While he wiped them on his napkin, his mind drifted to something not so sweet. Ray's pal (his dog) was sick.

Something in the pit of his stomach told him that he wouldn't have sweet Ponto very long. Ray's mind drifted to Ponto's only hope; he had to talk to Dad. Maybe he could get the vet to check her!

After the table was cleared, after the girls had done the dishes, and after Ray did the evening chores, a son went to his father for help. Meekly, the boy crossed the pasture in pursuit of his dad. Dad always seemed to be in a better mood in the late evening. When the sun is cascading colors across the Nebraskan horizon, illuminating the endless fields of corn, hearts are softened.

But Ray was wrong; this time he wasn't in tune with his father's feelings. For Bernice Beamer, this night was not his time of compassion. Berny's mind and heart were too centered on his disgruntled wife to have concern for his son's time of need.

Ray plodded through the grassy pasture and intercepted his father's path. Mourning doves' soft moaning added to the atmosphere of alarm.

With tight fists, words were finally spoken through Ray's thin lips. This was the time of decision.

"Dad, my dog's real sick," Ray gulped.

"I think .... I think she needs medicine. Maybe Doc Brenner or the vet could help me." Ray stared through his watery eyes at his father's face searching for a clue of mercy.

His son's voice pierced Berny's ears. His mind was way too fogged with the financial/marital problems that plagued his life. 'Not another problem!!' his mind screamed. How could he waste money on a dog, no less, when his family was five and his pocketbook less! He saw his son not nearly as tough as he felt a boy his age should be; he saw the tear Ray tried to hide. His mind made up, he spoke.

"Son, money doesn't grow on trees," Bernice stared straight into Ray's face. "Kill the dog. It'll make a man out of you."

"No, Dad. I can't..." Ray gasped. With his heart racing, his legs started racing, too. Thud! Something jerked him violently to a standstill. A hand, strong from farmer's work, blocked Ray's flight like a cement wall.

"Ray! Stop acting like a fool! You're eleven!" His father's voice was gruff, half-yelling. His bloodshot eyes were bulging at his son.

Tears streamed down the face of a heartbroken soul; he had to kill his best friend. Ray suddenly discovered a startling realization. At that moment, he was closer to his dog than to his father.

For a split second, he just stared at his father. No one understood him after all. He had no soul to help him; soon he would have to kill his one source of comfort and understanding that was visible to him.

"God understands me!!" he thought yet did not say aloud.

In a fog-like state that mimicked a nightmare, Ray felt himself follow his father into the barn. Flashbacks reminded him of happy times when he had thrown Mama's pancakes to Ponto; Ponto had loved pancakes.

His teary eyes saw his dog. He had been holding her only an hour earlier. The dog was still wrapped in the old brown blanket with which Ray had lovingly covered her. The honey-colored collie stared at him with excited eyes greeting her owner with a wagging tail that swished on the hay. Her eyes were excited to see her favorite master. Her pink tongue panted; she swallowed and tipped her head looking longingly into Ray's tear-filled eyes.

Ray couldn't bear it as he stroked her for the last time. He bent down and whispered in her ear. The fur dampened with his tears.

"I'm sorry, girl. Maybe I'll see you in Heaven. Right now, I wish I was there."

He picked her up, with the blanket still keeping her warm, and took her to the barnyard. She squirmed a little—but not much; yes, she was sick but she also was trusting. Trusting Ray, her pal, to do whatever he was going to do. With effort, she raised her muzzle to his face and licked it. He looked up at his dad. Slowly, he placed her on the ground where, only a few days earlier, they had played.

"Please, Dad. Maybe I could work at the General Store and pay you for the bill…... please, Dad," Ray's young boy's voice quivered.

"Listen, I know you really love this dog but you already are having trouble balancing school and chores. I think you'll agree with me when you are a man," he said as he handed the gun over.

Ray took the gun in his hand and backed up. He wiped the tears on his sleeve. Bringing the gun into position, he saw his dog's puzzled look when he didn't call for her. With heartbreaking effort, she started to get up.

"Shoot, son."

Ray killed the dog and ran away from her limp body. This time, his father didn't stop him.

— ❋ —

"How cruel," Hilda sighed as she reflected. "Enough of the memories for now."

The heavy-burdened old lady made her way over to her old roll top desk. Bills, like memories, just don't go away. After she had paid seven of them, she heard a familiar voice calling her name from the back door. It belonged to her close friend, to a fellow member of her church, to her neighbor of over thirty years. It belonged to Katy Den Hartog. Hilda scooted out from her desk and warmly greeted Katy at the silver screened door.

Chapter Two
COUNSELING IN THE KITCHEN WITH KATY

"Come on in! I have some sweet rolls left over from breakfast. Don't coffee and rolls sound good, Katy?" Hilda offered while trying to put a cheerful face on her tired one.

"You know, that does sound good!" the lady with softly curled brown hair, with hints of gray, agreed. Katy was larger than Hilda in stature though not larger in heart. Hardly anyone matched Hilda Virginia Beamer in her love for people. Katy was a wonderful lady and friend to many; Hilda and Katy were best friends.

With the rolls in the microwave, Hilda and Katy sat down at the kitchen table. The scene really hadn't changed over the years. They still sat at the same round, oak table. They still drank coffee. They still visited the way only old friends can. The only big differences were: They now were older. They now were wiser. They now were grayer. They now both had severe trials to face. Katy's Mert had M. S. and Hilda's Ray had Alzheimer's. Katy, having taken her seat, finally stopped to really study the friend she knew so well.

Hilda's gray hair was in disarray; no makeup graced her face. Her entire countenance displayed exhaustion. In fact, she looked literally unhealthy!

Her eyes were tired. Her face was pallid. Her smile was dulled. Her clothes weren't ironed.

Katy heard laughter in the den. There sat half-crazy Ray enjoying television! Ray appeared rested and really looked quite happy for his condition! The sacrifice of Hilda for Ray occurred so frequently that Hilda hadn't even realized the transition. With all of this on Katy's mind and heart, she turned and offered some sincere counsel.

"Hilda, don't you think that it is time to put Ray in a home? You are slowly killing yourself over his constant care. Please, honey, consider my advice," Katy's brown eyes half-squinted in deep compassion and love.

"I'll be all right, I just haven't been sleeping as well because of his crazy nights. Things will get better."

"They will, Hilda, when you put him in a home."

"How would you feel just putting Mert in a nursing home? You've been fighting his MS for a long time and you haven't given up."

"Well, I've felt like it at times but I've kept on with the Lord's and your help. But you know Hilda, I am fourteen years younger than you. And I don't have a heart condition like you do. I've probably said enough already, but I hate seeing your life waste away because of him."

"I know."

"How is Ruth Ann?"

"I hope that she's all right. She had a teaching job in Sioux City and something went wrong with the car. She said that a car repairman named Harry would take her home this afternoon; I guess since I don't know this 'Harry' I'm a little bothered."

"Ruth will use her best judgment. I would have gladly taken her home. I'm going into Sioux City anyway. Where is the car shop?"

"She didn't say."

"Well, if that ever happens again, you call me. Hey, do you need any groceries? I'm stopping at the grocery store when I get back from Sioux City."

"Ruth was going to get some this afternoon. But since I have no idea if she'll be able to, I think I'll take your offer. If it's not too much trouble, could you pick up a half gallon of skim milk? We're out and Ray just loves his

Raisin Bran," Hilda said as she smiled. Raisin Bran was his favorite cereal.

"But I'll pay you, Katy!" she continued stubbornly, nodding at the same time.

"Oh, no! Hilda, you've treated me so much. I'll treat you this time. Is it okay if I bring it past at about 1:30 PM?"

"That would be fine; I'm here all day anyway. I'll have to do something for you, though," Hilda said with a twinkle in her eye. No one could say that the Beamer's failed to reciprocate friends' kind deeds.

"Just being yourself is enough for me, Hilda."

The visit went on as usual until all the local news had been summed up. The neighbor across the alley had died, there was a new Victorian salon in town, and the large, new church building was almost completed. Then Ray started wandering.

Katy was about to tell a story about her granddaughter. However, when she saw him roaming toward the bathroom, Katy had to suddenly leave.

"I'll see you later on, Hilda. Try to take care of yourself!" Katy said raising her voice as she went out the back door.

"Okay!" Hilda half-hollered back as she walked toward Ray. Time for another bathroom battle.

— ❊ —

The kitchen sink was positioned directly under a window; it overlooked the Den Hartog's east side of their home and yard. This particular window was greatly appreciated.

Right now, Hilda was peering through it's small rectangle. She saw Katy slide into their older brown car and drive away; she was heading toward Sioux City. Then Hilda went back to her business. The breakfast dishes wouldn't wash themselves, so she was busily cleaning them. Ray used to help her dry.

After drying the dishes, Hilda discovered her next obligation was left undone. It was lunch time. Opening the refrigerator with a creak, she began surveying. Realizing how much food she really needed, Hilda was grateful for the milk she was expecting.

"Years ago, Katy would never have had to buy and deliver the milk," Hilda mused. Years ago, when so many things were so very different, the milk was delivered to their home. Hilda smiled to herself.

"Yes, the milk in the glass bottles...."

— ❋ —

"Ray! You're going to be late for work," Hilda said, but did not yell. After all, she never yelled at Ray anyway! And besides, if she had hollered, it would have rattled their little bungalow.

"I know. I'll be on my way, honey," Ray replied as he finished his orange juice and his last bite of Raisin Bran.

Hilda's house dress floated about the kitchen as she tidied up; she tried to keep their little home neat since she never knew who would "drop by." Being a new wife wasn't easy, but being a superintendent's wife presented new problems! One never knew if a special person would happen by or if teachers would "run past" some papers. But, she fit the part beautifully: She loved people and enjoyed the respect of her husband's position as superintendent of schools. She walked to the doorway to place the last empty milk bottle into the milk case for the milk man. She lingered—waiting to kiss Ray goodbye.

"Thanks for breakfast, Hilda," Ray smiled, wiped off his chin, and grabbed his briefcase. With his high cheekbones, brown hair, big blue eyes, broad back, sparkling smiles, and tall frame, Ray looked quite handsome—especially in his navy, pinstriped suit! There he stood—with briefcase in hand. Hilda felt proud.

"Oh, it was nothing," Hilda admitted as she cocked her

head in Ray's direction and sweetly smirked. She leaned against the door frame. He did look good.

"Did I tell you today that you look beautiful, Hilda?" Ray grinned as he met her in the doorway. He looked down into her eyes.

"No…. Not today…yet."

"Well, you are beautiful." Then, they kissed. They kissed goodbye for a long time…. Ray dropped his briefcase.

The brown, old clock on the living room table chimed. Only its bells brought them out of their "goodbye" kiss.

"You've got to go, sweetheart."

Ray nodded as he practically sparkled with romance. To look at him, one would have thought that he'd won the lottery! He grasped the handle and rushed onto the sidewalk and speedily strode to the nearby school office. Hilda gazed at her handsome husband of whom she was so proud. Then, after he'd walked about a half a block, she yelled, loudly!

"Ray! Ray!!"

With a jerk, Ray almost jumped in surprise and turned around to reverse. His face, open-eyed and startled, looked bewildered. Hilda shook her finger and pointed at his "briefcase."

He was carrying the milk case! Laughter ensued! There he, the superintendent of schools, had been hurrying to work with a milk case full of empty milk bottles for all the community to see! It was hysterical!

When Ray rushed up the walk to get his real briefcase, Hilda mused, "Maybe we shouldn't kiss goodbye—It's too much for you!" She giggled.

His cheery chuckle joined: "Maybe you're right!"

Soon they wholeheartedly resumed! But, he always double-checked himself to see whether he really had his briefcase….

— ❉ —

"Well, now Ray doesn't have to worry about that anymore........." Hilda bit her lower lip. Now, she was the one to worry. So many concerns crowded her life. Even grocery shopping—even simply buying some milk—had been affected by Alzheimer's.

"If Ray were well, we'd be grocery shopping right now," a little voice in Hilda's head said.

The memory of them visiting the grocery store would seem like a meaningless memory, but for Hilda and Ray, it had been a special time alone together—without the kids. They had enjoyed talking with the clerks. In fact, for most of the clerks, they were their favorite couple. Hilda would walk by Ray's side as they surveyed the new novelties. Going to the store meant discovering new items, going out to eat afterwards, and just being together. They were memories that were painful to remember. Just glancing into the den made the reality even worse.

Neither of them had ever seemed to tire of the other. *She knew that if she had been the one afflicted with Alzheimer's, Ray would be doing the same for her.*

It almost took away her appetite when she thought of the tragic disease afflicting him. But Ray's appetite was still good. He still hadn't hit the stage of half-starving, at least.

Walking to the patio, she was relieved to find a container full of some vegetable soup (that Ruth had made) still in the freezer. Slamming the old freezer door, Hilda headed back into the kitchen to defrost and to warm it.

When the soup was warm, she took it, (on a tray) and gave it to Ray. Then, Hilda sank into the sofa next to him and tried to enjoy her soup. He enjoyed the 12:00 PM local news. Hilda seemed to notice how much comfort he took in having her sit next to him. Years ago, she had always taken such comfort when she had stood next to him.

— ❋ —

Katy delivered the milk; Hilda did the dishes. Hilda

paid more bills; she helped Ray change. Now it was 4:30 PM; Ruth was not home.

If people were to have ridden past the Beamer residence, they would have observed an elderly lady hovering at the back porch window staring at her garage like a hawk. Hilda and Ruth really had become close because of Ray's disease. To infer that they weren't close before would be wrong. No one could dispute the fact that the Beamer clan loved and watched out for each other. Everyone in the family enjoyed Ruth's exciting personality. In fact, everyone in the family loved just being with Ruth. But, Ruth could forget things in her excitement.

With every passing minute, Hilda began to dislike 'Harry.' With every fifteen minutes, the pit of Hilda's stomach became deeper. With every passing hour, Hilda uttered a few more prayers. It was now 6:30 PM and Ruth was still gone. But Hilda's fears weren't gone. Would she ever see her daughter again? How she wanted to see her daughter! Her curly, short, mahogany hair, her face with beautiful high cheek bones, her large blue eyes and her perky expressions would be wonderful sights for Hilda!

"It's okay, Mama. Ruth probably just decided to go shopping for Christmas gifts since Christmas is coming up. December the 25th is only a few weeks away."

"You're right—but the idea of Ruth riding home with a strange man worries me. You would think that if she was shopping that she'd call me or something."

"Ruthy can be sporadic at times, though. Mama, all we can do now is pray. I've got to go take Carrie and Stacie down to the skating rink, otherwise I'd talk more. Call me when Ruth gets home, please. We'll all be relieved," Mary continued as she glanced at the stately grandfather clock in the living room. It struck 7:00 PM and the girls knew it.

"Thanks for talking, Mary. You tell the girls that my love is as big as the ocean and that I send them a kiss on every wave. Oh, and I will call you when she gets home."

"Thanks, Mom. I love you."

"I love you, too, Mary."

Talking to Mary somewhat comforted Hilda. But still, whenever headlights were seen outside the window, Hilda hoped.

— ❋ —

A large, old brown car pulled into the driveway. For Hilda, it was a welcomed relief. It was a tremendous blessing. It was an answered prayer.

— ❋ —

"First of all, I got you some really great gifts! But I won't tell you what they are! And don't peek!" Ruth smiled as she dropped some large shopping sacks on the kitchen floor. She clanged a mass of house keys, car keys, and other keys (for which their purposes were unknown) on the hook in the kitchen. Hilda gave her a hug.

"I am so glad you're home! What happened, honey?" Hilda sat down at the table and watched Ruth as she took off her jacket.

"The car didn't take nearly as long to fix; it only took a half hour. Well, Mom, I got to thinking about it and since the mall was across the street, I thought that I might as well drive across and go shopping. By the way, there is a really good Mexican restaurant at the mall and it just opened. I had some delicious burritos. I brought you both a couple. The cheese really makes them good!" Ruth threw the bag bearing burritos into the refrigerator.

"I guess there just wasn't an opportunity to call. Right?" Hilda was still so thankful that she was safe.

"I'm sorry, Mom. I really should have called. I guess I

I felt so loved, so proud, and so secure in Papa's strong yet gentle arms. We were such pals! (This is the photo of which I wrote.)

Aren't they a good looking couple? (Or am I biased?!) They enjoyed being color co-ordinated! Here they wore color coordinated Easter out-fits! They were so "spiffy"! Easter Sunday was wonderful!

The same day that Papa and I had our picture taken, we had this mo-ment captured. Carrie (my little sister) looks like such a darling! We were all ecstatic. It was Easter Sunday and Papa and Grandma were so proud to bring their only grand-children to church for all of their friends to meet!

was so stimulated with the excitement of getting gifts and stuff that it didn't cross my mind." Ruth looked remorseful as she leaned against the counter.

"It's all right. I will call Mary, though. Since it's 8:30, she should be home. And Ruth, we just care about and love you so much; please try to call me in a similar situation."

"I will, Mama. How was Dad?" Ruth said as she opened a pop can and poured some into a glass. She sat down across from her mother.

"The usual."

— ❄ —

Ruth could tell that her mother was wasting away and she felt like no one was stopping it. Ruth tried incessantly to help her parents. She had thought about talking to her mom about her personal insights; this was as good a time as ever. The conversation that followed was intense.

"Mom, Dad's not gonna get any better. Really, it almost seems like each week we lose a little more of him—and a little more of you. The care is just too wearing. It's pulling you down. We really need help! Did you call Lisa from the Alzheimer's Association about getting someone to change the bed and get Dad up for you?"

Hilda hesitated.

"Well, Katy came over. She bought us some milk, and I had to help your dad so much that I didn't after all. I guess I'll try tomorrow."

"See what I mean, Mom. You've said that before, maybe I'll have to call her myself."

Hilda looked down.

"You know how much I love you. We could do so many more things together if you'd only take some sort of action. We could eat at that special restaurant in Sioux City—Green Gables. And you know how much we like to shop. Please. Try harder," Thus concluded Ruth's half of the debate.

Try harder, try harder.... It seemed like each day Hilda felt like she had to try harder!

"What can I say more than that I'll try, Ruth? Each day is like a test. It's like Ray is the teacher giving me breaks as he pleases. Lately, he hasn't been giving me many breaks from his care," Hilda analogized.

The analogy represented her respect and obedience to him and his needs. But it also had a deeper meaning: Ray had been a well-respected teacher, guidance counselor, school psychologist, principal, and superintendent. Only now he had unknowingly taken over the classroom of Hilda's life.

"Listen Mom, I'll just take over this time and call her myself."

"Thank you for taking such an avid interest in me," Hilda said as her wrinkled hand gently gripped her daughter's smooth one.

"Sure, Mom."

"Anyway, how did your teaching job go?"

"I had to teach a talented and gifted class and there was a know-it-all kid. He was a real brat! He thought of himself not only as a genius on everything, but he was compelled to believe that everyone else should think of him the same way! Well, I certainly didn't think of him as an academic angel!"

She enunciated every poignant word. Ruth's eyes had become larger in exhilaration. They exhibited her frustration successfully.

"This *child* was only ten years old but he had the mouth of a rebellious teenager. He said that not only was *I* obnoxious but he continued to say (with the coolness of a snob) that *I* was a fake because I smile too much. Well, I had him in another class later that morning. When he walked in, I called him to my desk. As I smiled big and wide I said, 'I'll put your name on the board and tell your teacher on you if you cause any more trouble.' And he straightened up just like that!" Ruth said as she snapped her fingers.

Hilda and Ruth laughed.

"Shut up!" Ray exploded. His voice echoed from within the den. Alzheimer's spoke once more.

"Can't you people be quiet for a change?!"

The voice silenced the kitchen. The voice silenced the laughter. The voice rang in their ears. Words remained unsaid. They both knew. They both remembered. They both understood.

Alzheimer's causes its victims to be agitated because of many irrational reasons. At times, they are afraid and intolerant of people caring for them, people in general, being bathed in water, being left alone, eating dark specks in food, eating food in general, having their diapers changed, etc. And, indeed, noise is included. Sometimes they react with violence, defiance, crabbiness or loud outbursts. Loud outbursts were slowly becoming more frequent in the Beamer household.

The wallpaper in the kitchen was old. It had a brownish gold chain-like pattern that fell vertically to the floor elegantly covering the aged, ivory yellow background color with precision. Framed pictures of various sizes adorned the walls. Ruth was diligently, intensely staring at one in particular.

It was a picture of her dad at a time when he was younger, free of disease, and holding his firstborn granddaughter at Easter. They had been standing by the doorway to the den. He was smiling. He had worn one of his favorite spring suits. It wasn't a dark, stuffy-looking color. It was a pale, stylish blue. He was wearing his all-time favorite belt that had "Ray" inscribed with black letters on its large, oval, silver-colored buckle. His straight teeth were gleaming in the sunshine as he smiled with the little girl in his arms. He was so proud of little Stacie! She had worn a little white straw Easter hat with pink ribbons touching the lacy neckline of her mauve-pink, lacy, frilly dress. The picture had been taken in the den adjacent to the same kitchen where it now hung. The same wallpaper had been hanging then although it hadn't been as yellow as it was now. Their lives had yellowed, too.

The same man who had brought joy and unconditional love to his family now brought depression and relentless trials each day to them. The same man was sitting in the den recovering from his last outburst. The same man had silenced their happiness.

A whisper intersected the silence.

"Mama, sometimes, even though I know he's sick, he hurts my feelings. Even more frightening, sometimes it's hard to remember him the way he used to be," Ruth stammered in a whisper as she gazed up at the picture. The picture had frozen a happy time that could only be visited in memories. Sometimes the memories were hard to remember. Sometimes they were fogged by the constant stress and sadness. Hilda's eyes misted. All she could say was:

"I know. I hurt, too."

Ruth Ann hugged her mother. They didn't cry. They didn't sob. They knew that if they cried the tears would be uncontrollable. They just held each other.

Chapter Three
IN THE MOOD ...

Two hours passed since emotions had been churned. It was time for another stressful challenge. It was time to give Ray his pills. The two little soldiers were back at their post: the kitchen. It was time to decide on the strategy of their mission. It was an important assignment. If they didn't get the medicine down him he would be twice as likely to wander or run away. He would be twice as violent and twice as intolerant.

"Maybe if we dissolved it into some juice," Ruth contributed.

"Ruth, at bedtime?!"

"You're right."

"What if we crumbled and mixed it into some peanut butter; he will almost always eat peanut butter on bread."

"You know you might have something there." Hilda agreed.

"The only problem is that the Prozac can be crushed but the Aricept can't dissolve." Prozac and Aricept (a medicine specifically used to help Alzheimer's disease) seemed to subdue some of the symptoms. They needed any medical help they could procure. Ibuprofen is also used to help the patients.

"Okay, I'll go give him the peanut butter on some toast," replied Hilda receiving the command.

— ❄ —

The first plan was successfully completed. It was now time for an even more challenging maneuver: the Aricept.

Hilda gently wiped off some peanut butter from the corners of his mouth with a damp, pink washcloth.

"Ray, honey, it's time to take your medicine. It will make you feel a lot better."

"Oh," Ray said.

"Open your mouth, please."

"No," Ray said.

"But it would make us very happy, honey. Please, open your mouth."

A slow answer replied:

"Okay," Ray said. He opened his mouth and in went the pill.

"Now drink this water, please."

"Puh!" was Ray's reply as the pill launched out of his mouth and went spiraling to the floor.

The medicine cost way too much to throw away so Hilda rinsed it off at the kitchen sink. Within minutes Ray's mentality mellowed.

"Here, honey, please take this pill."

"Why, sure!" Ray said as he graciously swallowed. Ray looked up smiling from his deep rust colored chair. For Hilda and Ruth it flashed a little remembrance of earlier days.

"Thank you," Ray said.

Hilda and Ruth thought in unison:

'Thank You, God.'

— ❄ —

The clock struck 11:00 PM while Hilda was in the midst of beginning the most important segment of her day: devotions. She picked up the ancient family Bible.

Passed down from generation to generation of Hilda's

family, faith in the Bible was a foundation. Large, heavy, leather encased, and having been restored only once, it showed wear. Tucked inside the book, a reader would find family history. Yellowed birth announcements, frayed obituaries, blushing wedding announcements, glowing anniversary announcements, amongst other keepsakes. But the intricate Bible illustrations, interesting family history, and other important newspaper clips did not even compare to God's Holy Word.

Hilda placed it on her lap. She lifted the cover to awaken an old book smell and a crackle echoing from its spine. After paging through its fragile pages, she turned to the Book of Proverbs, Chapter 3. But her devotions did not continue as expected. After praying and reading the first segment, she carefully turned a page. Onto her lap fell a priceless newspaper clipping. It was her wedding announcement, discolored by almost fifty-seven years. About sixty years ago, a proud mother had tenderly clipped it for her younger child, her only daughter, her beloved Hilda.

Hilda looked at the clipping. She remembered her wedding so well—every little detail in the black and white picture aroused memories. Thus began a long, bittersweet walk down the worn old memory lane....

--- � ---

Hilda sat on the edge of her patchwork quilt draped bed. Mama had given the quilt for her twenty-fifth birthday. It had fabric of all colors—scraps from favorite childhood dresses and other nostalgic novelties. A chest, laid at the end of her bed, held many other objects of equal and greater significance.

Her bed was against the wall so that she could look out the window onto the farmyard bustling with chickens. The light, sun-bleached drapes dressed up the modest window of small proportion. She'd been thankful for it many times over the years not only because of the view, but also the breeze she gratefully welcomed on hot summer nights. Her desk was placed so that she could glance out the window while she graded her students' papers. A pile of papers signified her work was accomplished. Next to the desk, a dresser was located. Many grooming tools were arranged across the smooth, oak surface.

One powder puff box was special indeed. Her grandma (who died at the ripe age of ninety-nine and a half years) had given it as a high school graduation gift. An antique picture covered its silver, round top; little legs held the circular container upright. A whimsical tune played tin-like from its depths. Many times Hilda would sit near the dresser and listen to its sentimental melody.

Hilda wasn't listening to it now. She could have looked across from the bed and seen her reflection in its oval mirror, but she wasn't looking. All of her concentration happily centered upon one small object.

One diamond, gold ring adorned her left fourth finger; an engagement ring! She turned her hand back and forth in the sunlight; the sparkles reflected on the white walls.

"No ring of mine ever sparkled like this one," Hilda thought as she sighed with a smile.

She had many things to smile about! For merely two months Hilda would hang between being a Miss Hazen and a Mrs. Beamer. The majority of girls her age had young families of their own. But Hilda didn't fit into the majority. Hilda was Hilda!

Certainly she had had the chance to marry; her waiting for Ray M. Beamer to come along was more than just worth the wait. They were the perfect match.

— ❋ —

It was a night in the autumn of 1940. It was the night of the Harvest Dance. It was the night of Hilda's most promising encounter. No one knew what the evening held in its hands.

Leaves rustled outside Miss Hilda Hazen's window. Occasionally, leaves would fall onto the panes of glass from the towering trees. The sidewalk had become an autumn rainbow. Orange, yellow, brown, and red swirled together in the wind. The sun was lowering while beaming just enough light to capture richness of color.

Rays of sunlight spread across the book with

My! I certainly can see why Papa chose her at the dance! Can't you? She was pretty and so lovely ... And she certainly wasn't boring! She really got into the music! She had spunk!

which Hilda was curled up. Her mind was being thoroughly saturated in Philosophy; next Monday the professor had planned an exam. Her roommates were not interested in being little scholars.

Girls bumped and bustled, primped and rustled as Hilda read Philosophy. Incidentally, Hilda could not avoid being distracted—especially when one of them accidentally bumped her chair as she tried to put on her hose.

"Sorry, Hilda," Elaine apologized while she still tried to put her foot into the left hose leg.

"Are you positive that you have to study tonight? You've been pouring yourself over that book for hours!"

"I've been to other dances," Hilda paused, "but I think I've got a good enough grasp of the material for Monday. So I've changed my mind—I think I will go after all!" The spunky, fun-loving side of Hilda emerged once again!

"Great!" Lillian smiled and replied as she sat uncomfortably close to the mirror as she tried to apply make up.

— ✤ —

Three girls, with hearts beating quickly, entered the Dance Hall slowly. The dresses were their best—Elaine wore a delicate blue, Lillian a snowy white, and Hilda a soft violet. Only Hilda's had been a hand chosen gift from her doting father.

The parade of colors ended their walk near the punch bowl. No music was playing; they were the first ones who had arrived and the excitement was rather cold.

Then the ice was broken: the band started to play Glenn Miller's latest hit: *In the Mood.*

Hilda loved to feel the rush of Big Band and jazz. Apparently many others did, too. All of a sudden the Dance Hall and dance floor were being filled with the flow of jazz-crazed, ornate young people. Now the night was becoming exciting! Elaine and Lillian stood at the sidelines hoping for someone to sweep them out onto the dance floor. Where was Hilda? She had already been asked.

Ray had come with a group of the boys to get away from the stress and drudgery of college life. Only one of them had a date, and that certainly wasn't Ray!

Ray had seen her standing to the side looking sincere, excited, and lovely. He also concluded that she had a hidden liveliness about her when he side glanced at her purple bowed shoe tapping to the beat of the music.

Yes! That was the girl for him, he had solidly decided when he had peered down the line of stiff, tense young ladies; they were leaving an impression on no one but themselves.

So the tall young man, in an uncomfortable gray pinstriped suit, had found enough gumption to politely invite and gently guide the purple bowed shoes to the floor.

Swirled in the excitement of meeting a mysterious gentleman with beautiful teeth and dark brown hair, Hilda could barely withhold the swellings of exciting intrigue which eventually blossomed into a smile.

"My! She is beautiful!" Ray thought as he looked down at her pretty and captivating smile. His thoughts of captivation were interrupted, however.

"It certainly is nice to meet you...Mr. ...," she suddenly hesitated as she realized that she had no name to fill the blank! They whisked by a less flamboyant couple before Ray replied.

"Beamer's my name, Ray Beamer," he confessed as he gazed down at the illuminating sparkles shining from his dance partner's beautiful blue-green eyes.

"And I'm sorry. I guess I didn't catch your name either," he said a little more softly.

Her eyes sparkled more as she smiled once again.

"Hazen's my name, Hilda Hazen," she replied coolly, still continuing his distinguishing lingo of introduction.

They both smiled into one another's faces while simultaneously studying one another's features. Then clapping intruded their treasured privacy. Their first dance was over but their intrigue had just begun.

"Thank you for the dance," Hilda said as she joined in on clapping for the band.

"Believe me, it was a pleasure," he smiled. Someway one of Hilda's many acquaintances had found her; Barbara Rashner was her name. She, wearing a flamboyant red dress, rushed up to Hilda and in her self-centeredness, didn't notice Hilda's companion. Hilda

Aug. 20, 1940

Oh! To be in Lincoln!

Oh! To be in Lincoln
The Lincoln we all know
I'd like to be in Lincoln
In the evenings when the
lights are low.

Oh! To be in Lincoln
To visit all the parks,
And watch the copper
tread his beat
as soon as it gets dark.

Oh! To be in Lincoln
Some evening when it
rains,
The steady patter on the
streets,
Beats out its glad refrain

The neon lights in Lincoln
In Lincoln when its dark
Reflect like jewels
as you note
many radiating sparks.

Oh! to be in Lincoln!
Where I met the girl
I love.
Oh! to be in Lincoln!
when the stars are out above

Oh! to be in Lincoln!
when the moon is o'er the
lake.
We had such pleasant thoughts
we two.
It mattered not how late
it was growing late.

Oh! To be in Lincoln
Lincoln with all its
fun,
I shall remember dear old
Lincoln.
Till my work on earth is done
So here's to dear old Lincoln
In the summer of the year
We will all remember Lincoln
we salute you!
Lincoln, dear.
Ray M. Beamer

(Dedicated to H. V. Hazen
denoting the inspiration!)

This is a poem Papa quickly penned for his newly found sweetheart, my grandma. He would have surely recopied it had he known that I would include it in my book!

tried to be cordial. Barbara always enjoyed blabbering about her "private" romantic life. And of course, she immediately began jabbering about some new boyfriend. Her voice—with a heavy southern accent—formed a continuous sound.

"He couldn't bring me to this dance because he had to go home to see his ailing mother. I find that that is such a desirable quality in a man, that he would be willing to leave me to care for his poor, sick mother. I told him, 'Jimmy, don't feel bad about missing out on being with me. Honey, you go ahead and give your mother some care.'"

Few people could stand a few moments of Barbara's chatter. Hilda became desperate to halt the talk when she saw, in the corner of her eye, Ray reluctantly walk away.

"I thought that it was really rather noble of me, forsaking my own pleasure for his mother. He really felt sorry for me that I'd have to come to the dance alone. But I'm happy, Harry Hilkens brought me—but don't be jealous, now. You'll be asked out again some day," Barbara tapped Hilda on the shoulder as she jabbered and noticed no boyfriend standing next to her tolerant friend.

"But just don't be going after Jimmy," Barbara waved her finger at Hilda.

"He's mine!" Barbara gushed on and ended with an aggravating laugh.

All the while Hilda had said a few "Reallys" and "Ohs" in the midst of Barbara's constant conversation. Hilda actually hadn't soaked up very much information except that there was someone named "Jimmy" involved. All Hilda really cared about was Mr. Beamer, Ray Beamer.

"Well, Barbara, thanks for talking to me. I'll see you later," Hilda said as her eyes and head turned back and forth as she searched the crowd for the impressive gentleman. She made her way looking in every possible direction. Where was he? Finally, feeling defeated, she gave up and went to the punch bowl to drown her disappointment in the ruby-red, sweet liquid.

"Hi," a voice startled Hilda from behind to such an extent that she almost spilled the punch that she was pouring!

"Hello," Hilda turned around briskly.

"I'm sorry I left so soon, but I didn't want to intrude in your friend's conversation," he explained.

"She does talk—a lot," she admitted emphatically.

Thank God he'd come back!

"I guess we both like punch," he concluded. They both laughed.

— ❈ —

"So, do you have a large family?" Hilda was investigating his background. After all, here they sat enjoying a couple of shakes at the nearest cafe and really, she knew little about her companion!

"Well, it all depends upon what you would call large. I have two sisters, Mildred and Alice. And I did have a younger brother but I'm sorry to say, the hogs ate him!" Ray's eyes danced as he exhibited his slightly mischievous smile. Of course he knew that she wouldn't believe him.

Hilda tilted her head and gave a knowing look that showed her feelings of unbelief. Then, she straightened her head up and gave her best reply:

"I have one brother, Virgil; he escaped the hogs, thankfully."

They both laughed for they each had found their match.

— ❈ —

The perfect pair had now been dating for several months and it was becoming a serious relationship. This particular summer, Ray had been working extremely hard on summer jobs. He'd done so many painting jobs! Hilda, being her concerned self, had even told him not to work to such an extent. They hadn't been able to date as often because of his work schedule. Hilda was so happy that she would see him again. Ray had promised to take Hilda to the nearest amusement park. She enjoyed the park's rides and games immensely.

She now sat in a large white rocker on her parents' front porch waiting for his familiar blue car to pull into the long, gravel drive.

"My, I'm really glad that I chose this dress to wear on such a hot day!" Hilda said to herself. At least she thought that she was alone....

"I'm glad that you chose it, too. You look beautiful," her mother's familiar, comforting voice informed her. She softly spoke through the screen door.

Hilda smiled with a slight blush.

"Do you think that he'll like it?" Hilda wondered in earnest concern.

"He'll love it!"

"Thanks, Mama," she replied feeling a surge of confident excitement.

Hilda wore a lovely summer dress of a soft green. It complimented her fair complexion and brown hair so beautifully. It hadn't been merely Mother's flattery. Hilda looked marvelous! She appeared almost the epitome of modest, Christian beauty. What truly mattered, however, was not her appearance but her heart. Her loving heart was as pure as the white pearls adorning her neck.

Following the short discourse, Ray's vehicle quickly found its way into the driveway just as Ray had quickly found his way into the young lady's heart. Ray was so excited that he practically jumped out of the car. When his eyes located Hilda, Ray was dazzled.

"You look so wonderful!" Ray managed to say.

"Thank you, so do you!" Hilda replied as she saw the muscular, handsome man wearing a gray, dapper day suit. They were a striking pair. Simultaneously, they thought: *"There's the one of my dreams."*

After a magical moment of looking into each other's eyes, Ray took her hand and led her to the car. Hilda's mother waved from the porch.

"Mrs. Hazen, I'll have your daughter home by supper.

I'm really looking forward to your chocolate cake!" Ray politely spoke. Oh, no! He'd mentioned the cake!

"I wonder how he knew that we were having chocolate cake?" Hilda pondered....

— ❋ —

"My, I certainly had a fabulous time!" Hilda said as she glided into the car. She was beaming.

"I really did, too," Ray replied starry-eyed. He rounded the front of the car and slid into the driving seat.

"Even though it's later in the day it's still so hot!" Hilda voiced as she realized the heated atmosphere of the car. Hilda looked at Ray and noticed that he was gazing at her.

"Oh, my. What should I do? He's been acting a little different all day but I've never seen him look this way at me," Hilda thought to herself. For once, she couldn't think of a thing to say! But the decision was decided for her when he spoke.

"Hilda, honey, I truly love you and I want to spend my life with you. Will you marry me?" Ray tenderly took her hand.

Hilda's mind rushed. Her heart screamed **YES** ! but her mind was running at full speed: 'I can't marry him so soon! It's only the first summer after we met! I have to finish teachers' college, too!'

Finally, she spoke with joy-filled eyes. She heard herself say: "Yes, but not so soon. I have to finish teachers' college. Then... Yes!! I'll marry you!!"

Ray's eyes filled with incredible joy! His beam was as bright as the sparkling diamond engagement ring he slipped onto her slender left fourth finger. Hilda gasped!

"Ray! It's sooo... soooo.... beautiful! How could you afford such an outstanding ring?!"

"You know of all the jobs I've been working at this summer? It was all for my girl."

"I don't know what to say!"

"Your face says it all."

"I asked your dad for permission and that's why I knew about the cake," Ray explained as they looked into each other's eyes. They were so absorbed in one another! The awe filled the car with silence. Hilda didn't know what to do or say next.

"I think I'll open a window." Hilda slowly, softly said. Still looking into his eyes, she reached past Ray to open the window.

Whoosh! Ray swung her tenderly, gently into his arms and gave her a tremendous kiss which she never forgot.

Now, yes, now they were engaged!

Wedding bells were heard and dresses were worn. Hilda and Ray were wed. Hilda wore a stylish, sleek, size eight wedding dress that, though white, brought out her natural beauty. Ray's suit fit his broad chest and strong figure quite well. They were a pair to behold.

Their wedding was a wedding indeed! Her parents spared nothing, and it showed in the deluxe arrangements, refreshments (to which Hilda's mother had deliciously contributed), and the gala of delightful people.

No one seemed to remember the turmoil half a world away where Hitler was wreaking havoc. All that was bad was occurring in Europe while all that was good was occurring in the Tecumseh Methodist Church in little Tecumseh, Nebraska.

All attention from the ample refreshments, an assortment of flower arrangements, and August sunshine did not compare to the attention that Hilda received when she walked down the aisle. Everyone was shocked.

Hilda walked down the aisle alone.

Hilda's father was a passionate man who loved Ray tremendously. But, he just didn't like the idea of his baby girl marrying. Give his little girl away? Never! He felt so strongly against the fact that he had offered to give her any car she liked if she would just remain single! His feelings were often intense.

She had kept a smile on her face since it was her special day, but it still felt a little strange when she gradually glided past her sobbing father.

What a sight the Hazen couple made that day! Mr. Virgil Hazen soaked his handkerchief as he felt the crushing weight of his sorrow. His average sized nose was red. And his suit was being strained from his leaning over as he cried.

And then there was Mrs. Hazen, a rounder sort of woman shrouded in a navy blue dress; she had a kind, Christ-reflecting face.

Her mother was such a caring, joy-filled Christian. She never minded that Hilda hadn't married until the age of twenty-six. In the 1920s and 1930s, twenty-six was getting older to marry. Certainly her mother, Mary, had wondered a few times if Hilda would find that special someone; Hilda had known her heart and no one before Ray had set it on fire. At least, no one had until Mr. Ray M. Beamer entered her life. And Mary loved Ray.

Tightly permed, grayish brown hair encircled jolly eyes that had exhibited great joy when the engagement had been announced. Now they showed slight exasperation at the husband to whom she had been married for so long.

Patiently, Mary had tried to console him. When Hilda stepped by she had looked up at Hilda in dismay and even shown her a tolerant smile.

By the time the vows were exchanged, and the reception was under way, Hilda was so thankful and relieved. She observed her father getting along much better. In fact, he had an inverse reaction with Hilda's mother. In bringing Mary down in his sorrow, he had vented his feelings. He had strained her nerves! Now, he felt better but she felt worse!

All in all, it was a delightful day that had begun a delightful marriage. Had Hilda's mother not been there to console him, it might have been less than delightful.

Virgil and Mary Hazen—What a pair! Great-grandma was known for her <u>love</u> and <u>laughter</u>! Virgil was a doting dad! Just look at his sensitive eyes: He was generous but he'd <u>never</u> give <u>his</u> daughter away!

— ❀ —

Hilda just mouthed the priceless word only once—"Mama." She missed her mother's comfort when things seemed so sad. Hilda often wondered what consolation she would offer. But she knew her mother was celebrating in Heaven. Sometimes, when Ray had the worst of days, Hilda felt like it was the entire opposite of Heaven on earth.

— ✳ —

It was a cool, crisp, early winter morning. No one in the house was awake. At least, no one mentally capable. Only Ray occupied the darkly lit downstairs.

He struggled at the door. The outside beckoned him strongly. Only a small, brass, metal lock blocked his path; an easy lock for people of sound mind. But for an Alzheimer's victim, it might as well have been unconfessed sins that block an unbeliever's entrance into Heaven.

The lock was a cement wall to Ray; he desperately fought to get through it. He had the irresistible urge to get out, to do something, to find someone. The lock was so difficult to turn! He fought with it fiercely for a tense ten minutes. Then the lock subsided.

Freedom! Ray jerked the door wide open and felt the cold wind blow his hair astray. He clutched the out-door, metal, black stairway rail and lunged himself onto the sidewalk.

He limped and breathed heavily. A few snowflakes flew in the air melting on the ground, melting on Ray's bare head, and melting on the roof that covered Hilda's sleeping body a block away from where her husband now tread.

With every step and with every second, the wandering man became colder. Soon, his bewildered world became frightened. Where was Mildred? Where was Hilda? Where was Mama? Where was Ruth?

His eyes bulged and sweat froze upon his brow where it had fallen. In a state of panic, he began to limply do an elderly run. Where was Alice? Where was Mary? Where was home? Then, like an exhausted, hunted prisoner, he fell hard......

For some reason, Ruth woke up at about 5:30 AM, and she didn't know why. She sat up in bed and pulled on her old, green, slip-on house slippers. She yawned once and realized that a good glass of water sounded rather appealing. Mexican burritos made her thirsty.

Slowly, the well trodden floor creaked as she dragged her sleepy body down the endless hallway and into the night light lit bathroom. It was quiet.

The clear water, in a series of splashes, flowed into the clear glass. She gulped it down slowly and the coolness of the water slightly stirred Ruth out of her groggy state.

She walked over to the lowly set bathroom window and peered down into the dark yard.

'The snow finally is here. After all, it is December," Ruth drearily surmised as she observed the flakes fall steadily. She took another awakening gulp.

It was so quiet that she could hear her watch tick. It was too quiet. Something told her to check on her father.

She glided down the hall, much more awake and aware than previously, and noticed that his bedroom door was open. She rushed halfway down the staircase and stood at the third way landing. The door was wide open!

— ❄ —

Ray sat down on the curb. His forehead was bloody, his hands were forming thin scabs encased with dried, chilled blood, and his body shook from the mid-December cold.

"Whoever put me out here was stupid!" Ray uttered and shivered. He folded his arms to get warmer. At times, a car would go by with an individual who was either too afraid or too uncaring to halt and help him.

At about this time, a familiar old brown car began circling about the sleepy town with a familiar person driving. Of course, it was Ruth.

Her body was being pumped with adrenaline and her

heart thumped unmercifully. Her bloodshot eyes echoed the pain and fear from the depths of her heartbroken soul. Snow was falling at an increasing rate thus requiring her windshield wipers to begin squeaking into action. The streets were beginning to become slick with a coat of ice.

Ruth had no coat on just like her insane father! Insanity causes insanity, at times. Even the clothes she had sleepily slipped on were not appropriate for the cold weather! A pink T-shirt, old black jeans, and clogs were not destined for thirty degrees Fahrenheit! Thankfully, she had not cleaned out her car; next to her laid a blanket that she had snatched up at a garage sale. Slowing the car to a mere five mph, she tediously wrapped the blanket around her shoulders with one hand while the other hand steered the brown, long, old, vehicle. Only then, she continued on with her desperate search.

She scanned the streets and sidewalks making every attempt to be deliberate and conscious of even the minor details. If she saw a scrap of litter, it could be Dad's handkerchief! If she saw a teenager delivering the early morning paper, it could be Dad! A tree stump could be Dad piled on the ground. Every little questionable scene caused her car to slow down.

She came to a stop sign and bent her head (with brown, bed-messy hair) onto the steering wheel. She stopped and prayed an urgent prayer:

"Please, God, don't let Daddy get hit."

She decided to turn right. It was nearly three blocks away from home.

"How could a man, who barely gets up the stairs at night, manage to go this far by himself, no less!" Ruth said to herself as she tensely gripped the steering wheel harder until her knuckles became white as bone.

In her frightened state, she whipped around another corner sliding slightly on the ice paved streets.

She abruptly stopped to a standstill. For there, adjacent

to her right hand, sat a dismal figure whom she still called "Dad." Her search had stopped. Even the snow had stopped. But, Ray's pain and bleeding had not stopped.

Ruth pulled over about five feet behind her dad. Wildly, she practically leaped out so that she, too, became a part of Ray's tragic scene and mental turmoil. Then she made herself calm down. Her fearful state would only cause him to become more afraid. She approached him calmly and steadily. Her blanket, still disorderly wrapped around her shoulders, blew like a brown flag in the wind. Faced with an unbelievable situation, Ruth handled it well. She began with the perfect words whose strength fought the wind's.

"Hi, Dad. Let's go home."

"Yes, let's," Ray chattered as Ruth swung the blanket around his almost-hypothermic body. Ray was heavily leaning on her shoulder while tightly grasping her hand. Then, the daughter led her father to the car as they together fought both the disease and the cold wind.

— ❈ —

"My goodness, Ruth! You should have awakened me!" Hilda gasped as she stroked Ray's bandaged forehead with her caring hand.

"I'm sorry, Mama, I guess I just panicked. I would have gotten you up right away if I hadn't found him." Ruth defended as she sipped up her warm coffee. She reached over and straightened her dad's electric, light-blue blanket around his feet.

"Well, are you both warm now?" Hilda worried aloud as she tried to cover Ruth with another quilt and Ray another blanket.

"We're doing well… now. He looks like he lives in the winters of Alaska with all of the gloves and layers I dressed him in! I dressed his wounds and gave him a bowl of soup—this is his third bowl! And don't be upset, he has no symptoms of hypothermia or any broken bones. The cuts are going to need careful attention but, thank God, they aren't serious. Otherwise, the only thing that we are both suffering from is fatigue," Ruth proclaimed as she heaved a loud, strong yawn. Fully surrendering to her exhaustion, Ruth slid out of her sitting position and flopped across the sofa.

"Honey, I just don't understand how he could have gotten out! Tell me again: How far was he from home?"

"Well, I guess it was about four blocks North. I couldn't believe it. He isn't a fourth of the man physically or mentally that he once was! He must have just enough left in his brain that he could figure out how to unlock the door. I told you to call someone to get a new lock for Alzheimer's people last week, Mom!"

"I know," Hilda answered as she realized that Ruth's exhaustion was causing her to become crabby. Ruth's face had formed a tired frown.

"Maybe we could watch some television. I need something to help my stress level," Ruth managed to say between yawns.

"Whatever you want, honey," Hilda said in a comforting voice.

"Ray, sweetheart, do you want to watch some TV?"

"Yes, that's fine," Ray's elderly voice weakly replied as he fell asleep.

"Well, you just tell me if you want anything else. I'll be in the living room reading the paper," Hilda explained as she turned on the television with the silver remote.

Crackles echoed from within the living room as Hilda turned the newspaper's pages. Every once in a while she would glance in to see the two warriors asleep as the television blared the early morning shows. A 6:30 AM fishing program, unbeknownst to the slumbering den audience, had just ended. Now a more lively program began to start.

Hilda heard the theme song with which the entire Beamer family was acquainted: the opening song of

Gunsmoke. She couldn't help but remember what a different scene it would have been at a different time.

— ❀ —

They all began the program with everyone singing the theme song together. Little Ruthy, sprawled at her father's feet, watched intensely; her eyes danced in excitement. Her hair stuck out in shiny bunches that peeked out from beneath a red cowboy hat. She even wore little cowboy boots that Mary had physically outgrown but emotionally still loved.

Mary had on a little halter with two little red guns. A blue cowboy hat sat upon her fluffy blond head. Though the sisters both liked "Gunsmoke," they differed in the extent of how wild they became during "extra exciting parts." Ruth sometimes would jump up and down if a bad guy was coming. Or Ruth would throw her arms about bing-banging her guns at the bad guy. It certainly was no surprise that Mary sat at a safe distance from her sister; but she, too, became enthralled in the program.

Ray sat in the recliner that rocked back and forth during the show; sometimes it rocked more quickly when there was a chase. In a way, the chair was Ray's horse. Really, he still was a young cowboy at heart.

And then there was Hilda sitting next to her husband. She enjoyed the show well enough; though romance movies were more to her liking. But there were times when she even shot at the bad guys!

— ❀ —

Hilda couldn't help but compare the contrasting scenes. Ruth wasn't jumping up and down. Mary was at home with her husband and two girls. Ruth didn't shoot at the bad guys. Mary was in bed in Cherokee, Iowa. Ray's injured body didn't rock his chair with the horses. Hilda wasn't at his side. Instead, it was best described as this: Ruth was asleep. Ray was asleep.

Chapter Five
THE CALL

Hilda tossed and turned; sleep wasn't coming easily. The entire day had started and ended horribly. First, he ran away; then the day was spoiled by his outbursts. Really, Hilda wasn't as upset over the outbursts. She was upset because of the source of them. Alzheimer's disease. Why did her Ray have to suffer so?

In many ways, the disease had caused him to deteriorate almost to the extent that he looked like a different person. He was the skeleton of the man he once had been. His hair had grayed severely. His whiskers protruded in various directions from his face and ears due to lack of shaving. His eyes had withered from a lively, clear blue to a dull, cloudy gray. Having refused the brushing of his teeth many times, Ray's teeth were decaying.

What had been white, now was yellow. What had been strong, now was weak. What had been polite, now was rude. What had been Ray, now was Alzheimer's.

"Oh, come now Hilda! There are worse ways to die," Hilda confided to herself as she pictured her frightful husband. She snuggled down into the comforting yellow sheets and covers. She paused.

What worse way was there to die? After giving it some serious consideration, she discovered her answer.

"Thank God he doesn't have cancer. Chemotherapy makes patients suffer so much," she passionately pondered.

Hilda shuddered to think of how many friends and relatives she had lost to cancer and other diseases over the years. Even her close nephew Richard. It was so hard for Hilda to believe that the little baby she had cuddled and cared for had grown up, had even been a grandpa, and had died. In fact, because of cancer and other causes, she had outlived not only both her precious nephews (Richard and Donald), her priceless brother, and her loving parents, but had outlived also countless cousins. She was the last Hazen living from her immediate family. She, and her ninety-four year old sister in law, Ruth Hazen, were the matriarchs of the Hazen side.

After she had solemnly remembered all the people she had grieved over so much, she fought insomnia all the more. It was little wonder that she could not sleep.

— ❋ —

"Good morning, honey," Hilda exclaimed as she met her daughter in the kitchen.

"Hi, Mom." An exhausted Ruth droopily gazed up at her mother's compassionate face. Her eyes had circles so dark that they looked like the reflection of the coffee she was now drinking. A dark mood presided over the kitchen table which had known so much laughter.

"Well, I might as well tell you. He kept me up since 3:00 AM," Ruth confessed in a hoarse, morning voice.

"Oh, honey! I'm so sorry," Hilda softly said with a mother's tender, loving care.

"Next time, please wake me—after all, you have teaching jobs—I only take care of Ray," Hilda continued as she patted her daughter's shoulder with her gentle hand.

"I think that there are times that you work harder than me. You have a much more stressful job than I do at times," Ruth admitted as she sipped her strong coffee.

Hilda remained silent, but inside she felt the same way.

"Really, Mom, it's like you have the job of a full time nurse, and you are eighty-four…and with a heart condition! Good grief, Mom! I don't know how much more you can stand this…let alone me!" Ruth raised her voice with intensity as she elaborated.

She jerked her weary head as she spoke and glared into the den where the object of their care now reclined. As she stared at her father, her eyes brought forth a few tears as her soul silently cried out to God. 'Please, Christ, help my mother and me!'

Ray had always come to his little girl when she cried if Hilda wasn't there. Whether it was because of a dropped ice cream cone or a stinging remark made by another child, he had comforted her with a big fatherly hug. Nothing seemed too overwhelming when Daddy's strong arms surrounded her and her problems. He had been there. But now, he wasn't there to wipe away her tears; he was the source of her tears for the very first time.

Suddenly, gentle arms wrapped around her and a gentle voice, a quivery voice soothed,

"I'm so sorry…and I'm sure…he would be, too."

Hilda could barely stand the sorrow which hung over the household everyday. In fact, she was surprised that she hadn't been the one to cry first.…

Later that same week, Ruth made her escape. She went Christmas shopping. Hilda stayed at home. She finally slipped into the kitchen to phone Lisa Niebuhr, an Alzheimer's Association's social worker, while Ray slept deeply. It was the call Ruth had wanted her to make weeks ago ….

The table was chock full of take out bags that exhibited "Freddy's Foods" on the brown paper. Hilda sat across from Ray and Ruth. Ketchup decorated the corners of their mouths. Cheeseburgers were clamped inside their hands. It was a good meal.

"Thanks again, Ruth. Everything is great!" Hilda smiled as she tried to make things better than they truly existed.

"Well, I am glad you think so, Mom," Ruth said in a somber, low voice for she was in a depressive mood. Even though she had done some fabulous shopping, she still had to come home and face her family life. She felt like her life was going nowhere. Hilda knew her daughter well. She caught the mood that Ruth was immersed in and fought it with some good news.

"We're going to have some help."

With just those few words, Ruth's spirits began to lift.

"When, Mom, when?" Ruth looked at her mother in almost an awestricken stare. She had called Lisa Niebuhr after all!

"Next week, on Wednesday at 10 AM. Is that okay with you?" Hilda smiled as she saw a spark enlighten her daughter's eyes for the first time in quite an interval.

"Of course!" Ruth exclaimed. But when she turned her head to her left, she noticed her father becoming more tense with her loud outcry. She lowered her voice as she watched his clouded face.

"Of course, that's all right with me," Ruth's much lower voice repeated.

"I thought that it would be," Hilda winked.

Suddenly, the telephone rang.

"Go ahead, Ruth. Pick it up in the den. I'm quite sure that you'll want to receive this call," Hilda smirked.

Placing her napkin on the table, Ruth rushed into the den with the excitement of a child.

"Hello," Ruth greeted as she plopped onto the sofa.

"Hi, honey. How are you?" It was Lawrence. Lawrence from Texas. Lawrence from Ruth's romance. Lawrence— with the black hair and kind heart. Lawrence. The man to whom Ruth had been engaged, the man with whom she so eagerly spoke.

"Well, things are terrible! Dad's gotten much worse since you moved to Texas. We are finally going to get some help next week. But other than that, I don't know what we're going to do. Mom just can't let go," Ruth spoke in a half-whisper.

"Hilda's always thought of others more than herself," Lawrence replied in his soothing Southern drawl. Then he said the sentence that made Ruth feel extra giddy inside:

"I've missed our conversations."

"I…have, too."

"We'll have to talk a lot more."

"Oh, but the rates are so high!"

"No, honey, what I meant was when I come to visit," Lawrence replied as he revealed his secret with a huge smile.

"You're coming back to Iowa?!!!" Ruth exclaimed. This time she didn't care very much when her father's voice from the kitchen yelled: "Shut up!"

Laughter echoed from the receiver. Ruth's excitement amused him.

"Yes, I'll be coming in about seven months. I'll come stay a week or so. June 26, 1999, I suppose. It'll be hard to wait. It will be a long seven months, too. Believe me."

"I don't care how long it'll be, just as long as you come. You know that I'll be looking forward to it. This is truly wonderful," Ruth replied softly. Now this would give her something to hope for!

"Well, dear, I'm sorry to keep this so short but I've got to go to work early, which means I've gotta go to bed early."

"You sleep well, honey. Good night."

"Good night."

Ruth slowly placed the black and white phone on the receiver. She grinned. Lawrence was coming!

Hilda was still eating her cheeseburger in the kitchen when she overheard Ruth call Mary to tell her the new, uplifting news. However, it wasn't new information for Hilda….

While Ruth had gone shopping that afternoon, Hilda had unlocked the secret during a call with Lawrence. Almost immediately after she had called Lisa, the phone had chimed. The conversation was pleasant because of the undeniable fact that both parties liked each other well. By the end of the visit, Hilda knew her assignment.

She had agreed to let Ruth answer the phone at exactly 6:30 PM. It had been hard to keep the secret a secret. But it was worth the wait to just hear Ruth become excited and joyful again. In fact, she couldn't help but notice Ruth's extreme excitement over her ex-fiancé. This time, Ruth was ecstatic, but other times she had been less than overjoyed with Lawrence. Hilda began to think about the ups and downs of their romance....

Reflecting upon Ruth and Lawrence's bond meant recalling a long complex drama. Their's was an unpredictable paradox: Their confusing closeness, their aggravating arguments, their not-so-curt courtship, their engagement, their broken engagement, and their reconciliation.

Hilda had always tried to be there for Ruthy but there were times that even Hilda was confused about their relationship. There had been times when Ruth and she had talked well into the night following one of Ruth's dates.

It had been quite the anthology when he had lived in Iowa. Sometimes, Ruth would be in the clouds! Other times, Ruth would be below sea level.

Somehow they had grown through their experiences— good and bad. Hilda had been with them every step of the way.

Chapter Six
SHARING INSANITY, SHARING CEREAL

"Just a little further!!" Ruth half-yelled, half-gasped.

"Come on, Ray, put your foot up on the stair and take a step like this," Hilda then demonstrated.

His clouded face exhibited no understanding. He just stood there—rather—leaned there against Ruth and Hilda. Their instructions were so incomprehensible that they might as well have spoken in a foreign language. Astute Hilda saw what was occurring. He didn't understand. She tried a different, simplified approach

"Foot.... up-" She said. Ray turned his weary head and his fogged face looked at Hilda's stressed one. He seemed to grasp a little of the meaning. He moved his foot.

"Yes! Yes, now 'up' on step."

He put his foot on the step—and slipped! He began to fall! Ruth barely caught the big, heavy man. She maneuvered his fall into a sitting position. Now, they had to find another way to get him up.

For one hour, they had attempted to take him upstairs to bed. They had tried to have him sleep downstairs but he refused. Explaining, demonstrating, and allowing him to lean on their shoulders were all part of the process. It was unbelievable. It was unbelievable to think that he was able to walk easily just a couple hours earlier. It was unfathomable to think that he did not seem to grasp their simplest instructions. And now, after all their efforts, he had ended up sitting on the stair with a blank, tired expression.

"Now, listen, Dad. You've got to go to bed. To sleep.

Now, get up and let's go up the stairs together. We're here for ya."

He folded his arms. His blank face looked as though his mind had vacated

"Come on, Dad." Ruth sat down next to him.

"Here, now, let's scoot." She scooted up one step.

"Now you do it, Dad."

He sighed.

She got up and came down a few steps so that he looked down at her and she looked up at him. She patted one stair and then patted the next as she said:

"Move, up."

Not a wave of understanding crossed his countenance.

"Butt…. up." He gave a side glance at Hilda and then scooted up a step!

"That's the way! Keep going, honey!" Hilda encouraged. He was on a roll until he came to the third step from the top. Then, he ceased movement. He proceeded no more. He sat still. No matter their pleadings, he sat still for a long time: two, long, exasperating, tiring hours.

Hilda couldn't take the boredom. She was tired; Ruth was stressed out. Ray was seated.

She walked carefully past Ray. Hilda grabbed a desk chair from Ruth's room and sat down at the landing. She straightened up, gazed down at her weary comrades, and folded her hands. They both looked up at her.

In a dignified voice, she spoke. "The meeting will now come to order."

Even in the midst of such outlandish circumstances, Hilda still had her sense of humor! Even Ruth and Ray laughed—though Ray didn't understand why. (In fact, having a meeting at midnight on a stairwell would have seemed normal to him!)

— ✳ —

One hour later, Hilda and Ruth yielded. They called

the police. After all, whom could they call at one in the morning? Ray was a huge man and they weren't strong enough to lift him. They even feared for Ray's safety; he was precariously perched upon a high step.

The police were wonderful; they came by, lifted him up, and placed him in bed. Later in the week, Hilda decided, she would send cookies to the police department for their kindness. But, their horrible night was not over. In fact, it had just begun....

It was now late at night—a time when every normal person should be in bed asleep yet steps were heard. Steps rampaged down the upstairs hallway. Heavy steps, limping steps, Ray's steps resonated throughout the entire upstairs. Unfortunately, all occupants heard them.

Up and down the hall they went encompassing the second floor. Endless mental turmoil kept Ray stomping. Endless stomping kept Hilda and Ruth awake. It was unbelievable that he was able to walk with such spryness and ease when an hour earlier, he couldn't move an inch.

After fifteen minutes, at 2:30 AM to be exact, they stopped. They had halted at Hilda's still closed door.

He knocked hard. Quickly, the door crashed open in direct response to his pounding. Hilda saw the towering shadow of Ray, the now mad man, standing in the doorway. The only light, from the hall, streamed in through the door in the dimly lit, quiet bedroom.

"Alice, it's time to get up!!" Ray yelled. He stood motionless as he gave a crazed glare at the figure in the queen-sized bed. Hilda prayed for patience. Then, she slowly turned over in bed to face him.

"Ray, it's two-thirty in the morning. Please, go to bed; we all need our sleep," Hilda drearily said as she sighed a deep sigh. For a moment, it seemed to appease Ray. But, alas, he became angry.

Hilda's patience was rewarded with a slammed door and frightful, wandering footsteps. She heard Ruth's door opened and the similar, sad scene replayed. Only this time it had a happy ending. Hilda could hear Ruth yawning as she told her father what to do:

"Please,...for my health's sake, go to bed."

"Well,...a...okay." He turned around, clamored across the hall, and went to bed. Hilda heaved a deep sigh of relief and snuggled under the covers to get some much needed rest. For a wonderful two hours, she slept a deep, dream-filled sleep. It was to be all of the remaining sleep she would receive....

Stomp! Stomp! Stomp. Stomp, stomp, stomp. Hilda awoke as the steps echoed and trailed down the hallway. Hilda simply, sleepily said to herself:

"No, not again!"

Then the steps halted at Hilda's doorway again. The same figure stood shadowing the doorway, again. The same tired, crazed look stared at Hilda in the bed, again.

"Mary! It's time to get up!" the familiar yell resounded.

"No, Ray, It's 4:30 in the morning. We all need our sleep. Please! Go to bed."

"I need some breakfast. It's time to get up!"

By now Ruth had been stirred and she stood yawning behind her dad. Knowing that this time he would not be convinced of slumber, Ruth rolled her eyes in exhaustion and gave up the fight. Looking as exhausted and exasperated as possible, Ruth folded her arms and surrendered.

"Come on, Dad. I'll fix you some lunch...I mean breakfast." She yawned again.

"Does cereal sound good to you?"

"Oh, I don't give a darn either way!!!" he angrily answered breathing heavily in his unreasonable fit. Hilda could see sweat on his brow dripping down his furious face.

Ruth looked in at her mother for guidance. What should she do?

"Ray, you go ahead with Ruth. You like Raisin Bran, honey. Go on down with Ruth and have some cereal." Hilda almost always seemed to be able to soothe Ray like no other person. A comforted expression crossed Ray's entire countenance. He sighed with a slightly perplexed face.

"Okay," Ray answered slowly yet slightly calmed.

So, teddy-bear-pajama-clothed Ruth placed her hand on his burgundy-pajama-draped shoulder and wearily guided him down the staircase....

Hilda couldn't sleep knowing that Ruth was suffering downstairs. She slowly sat up in bed and fished for her glasses on the night stand. With her eyes half-open, she slid on her pink slippers which her loving grandchildren had given her, and tightly wrapped her purple robe around her sleep deprived body. Hilda druggily made her way out the illuminated door....

"Come join us!" Ray (the host transformed) greeted, smiling a toothy grin. There he sat perfectly peaceful, perfectly patient, and perfectly polite.

"Thank you, Ray," Hilda replied immersed in the bewilderment of the moment. She pulled out a chair with a creak to sit adjacent to her husband.

"Sure," he answered, still in an acquiescent mood.

Could this be the same deranged Ray that had just minutes ago rampaged the upstairs? Hilda just shook her head in a state of dismay as she stared at her husband's smiling face.

Undeniably, it was 4:40 AM! Unquestionably, they had only three hours of sleep! Unequivocally, they had no choice! They were the perfect example of two souls trying desperately to make a lemonade out of an old lemon.

"Would you like some cereal, yourself, Mom?" Ruth offered. Ruth stood near the cereal cupboard awaiting her mother's reply.

"Why, not?!" Hilda exclaimed with a lot of enunciation as she patted the table. Even though the sun had not risen, the threesome sat together sharing fatigue, sharing insanity, sharing cereal.

White flakes floated from the sky like a fluffy, white

sheet gently draping itself over the entire city of Le Mars, Iowa. Brick buildings became towering igloos and ordinary yards became winter playgrounds. Frost coated the windows like white paint on an artist's palette. Roads became ice rinks where cars began to slide. Assuredly, winter had arrived.

Snowflakes descended from the sky like problems descended upon the Beamer household. It had been two weeks since Lawrence had called and Christmas was only a week away. It was supposed to be a joyful celebration, yet, various shadows darkened the holidays.... Ruth finally got the nerve to pull out the heavy, complicated Christmas tree. She refused to allow the disease to take away Christmas! She, herself, tediously decorated it with silver garland, multicolored lights, sparkling tinsel, and priceless ornaments that now had become heirlooms (her favorites were the bubblers—when they heated, their colorful liquid went up and down). Finally, Ruth climbed a chair to reach the top. She placed the star.

She had no father to help her put the weighty tree up; no Dad to hang the star. Her dad had always put the star on the top. Even Christmas was affected by Alzheimer's.

By the time Ruth had finished the insurmountable Christmas tree, she was more spent than before. After stepping back to survey her work, she found it to just not be the same. In fact, everything just wasn't the same. It hadn't been the same for many years—ever since the beginning of the fatal disease. Ruth found herself drinking a large glass of refreshing water as she looked back in time to the beginning of her father's demise.... The beginning symptoms of his fight with Alzheimer's....

Chapter Seven
WHAT? NO GARDEN?!

For years, Ruth had toiled in, taught for, and treasured the town of Stuttgart, Arkansas. It had been a difficult separation for her to be so far from home, but she'd found (as she was accustomed) many faithful, fabulous friends whom she would never forget. The South had treated her well but no one could fill the shoes of her parents. They understood her more than anyone else in the world. Now Ruth was moving up to her homeland: the North. It came as no surprise that after three, whole years of teaching at the Christian school in distant Arkansas, Ruth was heading home.

Two anxious little girls, their mother, and grandparents sat in the airport's waiting terminal. Stacie was an excitable, outgoing six and a half and Carrie was a shy, mother-clinging four year old. The two nieces with light brown, fluffy hair, felt that the plane "was way too slow to come down!" Many times the inquisitive, aunt-loving little girls would ask:

"Mommy! When is she coming?!" Pretty soon, a young voice would ask again: "Grandma! Papa! When is she coming?!" Pretty soon, even the adults felt like flight 777 was incredibly slow to land. When the two dressed-up little girls heard that the plane had landed, no one could stop them from cheering. When people began to file out of the plane, the little girls would ask:

"Is that one her?!" When the polite, though anxious,

They celebrated their 40th anniversary with friends and family. Don't they look like they are having fun?! Little did anyone know that within the decade youthful Ray would begin treading the dreaded Alzheimer's disease's path.

small children asked the question five more times, the adults, too, felt impatient and incredibly enthused! Then, the last person to get off of the plane rushed into the airport with a belted, big, brown bag thrown across her slim shoulders. Finally, the trim, tall, pretty young lady met her family near the baggage terminal. Suddenly, she was surrounded with love and clinging nieces.

It was 1991. It had been a good flight. It had been a good day. Aunt Ruth was home.

It wasn't too long after her homecoming that Ruth had noticed some changes in her dad. He was sleeping more. He was forgetting more....

"Ruth! Where are my car keys?" Ray asked as he threw his voice up the stairway. Ruth walked out of her bedroom and started down the stairs to intercept him.

"You had them last night—remember? You put them on the counter in the kitchen." Ruth said as she leaned on the thick, oak banister and looked down at her dad.

"Goodness! I guess I just forgot," he exclaimed as he shook his head.

"Thanks, Ruth."

"Sure," Ruth quickly made her way down the stairs and stepped by him. She had answered in a confused voice that fit the puzzled look that had crossed her face. His question wouldn't have struck her as being strange had it not been the second time that he'd asked....

Soon after the key incident, Ruth had noticed that her dad wasn't keeping up on current events. For over a week, they had planned to eat lunch with Katy and Mert....

The couple sat in the den with the morning light pouring over the papers that they read. Hilda looked smashing in her turquoise sweater and pants. Her brown hair had been carefully fluffed to encircle her face with the greatest precision. Gold hoop earrings and a gold cross necklace finished off her meticulous appearance. She fit well with Ray's scrupulous ensemble. He wore black pants (with his famous "Ray" belt) with an ironed white shirt and red vest. His hair was combed without a hair out of place. His face was handsomely well shaven and he had wonderful, spicy aftershave which he never neglected to wear. They both were well prepared for the day even though they were just reading the morning paper! (It was interesting to note that the previous night they had stayed up late just to watch a romantic movie! Ray and Hilda were romantic even after forty-nine years of marriage!)

"Hilda," Ray began as he peered over the newspaper in the den. He looked straight across at Hilda who was enjoying another section of the paper.

"When are we going to have lunch with Mert and Katy?"

"At 11:30, dear," Hilda answered as she leisurely sipped some coffee.

Papa Ray and Grandma Hilda were always very affectionate. People often remarked about how remarkably close they were. (Here he is wearing the little Khaki cap which I describe.)

Ruth had been in the kitchen getting some cereal for breakfast; she had been able to hear every spoken word in the den.

When she heard him ask her mother about the lunch, Ruth drew in a sharp breath. She felt her heart begin to beat a little more quickly. A seemingly casual question had a seemingly tremendous impact.

"Why'd he ask her when he just asked me?" Ruth whispered to herself in shock. She walked backward and leaned heavily on a counter in the dark portion of the kitchen. Her mind raced as she searched for answers.

Could he just be too tired? Was he losing his hearing? Wasn't he concentrating? However, there was another question that loomed in the back of her mind. She shunned it passionately and fought its possibility until another incident brought it out into the open....

After Ruth had been home about a month, the strangest event took place: He gave up the garden.

For over twenty years, Ray had taken such pride in his property, his yard, but especially, his garden. For hours during the week, he would water, plant, and fertilize. Besides having a lawn like a luscious Persian carpet, his garden was almost impeccable.

His favorite friend was Miracle Grow. His tomatoes were fantastic: plump, round, red, and juicy. His beans were tender and green. And his berries! Farmer's market couldn't surpass their bountiful supply of sweetness!

Why, then, would a man so heavily involved in his hobby, suddenly drop it? That was the very same question Ruth asked when he announced his gardens' termination....

They had been standing next to the garden. Ray was in his old denim jacket with the rip at the collar. For some reason, for years the farmer in him loved the jacket and the idea of working in the garden that he loved so well. He had a little khaki cap. A blue, perky short set clothed Ruth's body. Its style contrasted with the garden man's. They may not have been sharing tastes, but they were sharing the beautiful spring day.

Leaning against the hoe, Ray made his plunging announcement to his perplexed daughter:

"You know, Ruth, I'm not so sure that I can keep up with this garden at my age."

He looked out over the garden and the lawn covered with dancing rays of sun. As he swallowed hard and stared at the products of his labor-filled, love-filled hobby—he had sort of a distant expression. It was as though he wanted to continue yet something or someone was stopping him.

Ruth looked up from where she sat on the back porch's concrete steps. Before the conversation had begun, Ruth had been mulling over her dad's peculiar behavior. The statement "You know, Ruth, I'm not so sure that I can keep up with this garden at my age" made her mental turbulence a hundred times worse.

There she saw a dad who was completely capable physically to maintain a large garden—maybe even a larger one.

"But you love it, Dad! You aren't that old at all! Age has never been a factor for you. After all, you were an older man when you and Mom had me," Ruth replied in earnest. The garden was so valued—how could he even consider it?

"You're sweet, honey. I'm glad we had you even though we were older parents," he admitted as he stooped and gave her a kiss on the cheek.

"I'll have to think about it. It's just so much work." With a searching look, Ray went inside to take care of the trash.

As Ruth sat outdoors, the spring wind wasn't the only thing turning things around. Ruth's mind churned and shook the circumstances until she found no other question that fit the situation and symptoms. "It" would be a disturbance that would plague her mind thereafter. Then, she asked herself one of the most poignant questions that every grown child fears most. It is the question that terrifies if the answer is positive. The question was so fierce that it heated her tongue as she whispered it: "Does he have Alzheimer's?"

— ❊ —

Now the answer was dramatically revealed. The passivity (a dramatic behavioral change) was a symptom of the early stages of Alzheimer's disease. By now, Ruth was on her second glass of water and with it came a second realization for Ruth to ponder. (Nervousness prompted the second glass—not thirst.) It seemed like, even in the beginning stages of Alzheimer's, Hilda had been in a state of denial.

In some ways, the symptoms of Alzheimer's had been in a masquerade when Ray was with Hilda. They had been able to talk about old times and memories in which Ray could easily join. Hilda had easily dismissed minor mistakes in daily life as "just old age." However, she had noticed that she had to give him directions to the grocery store. She had had to help with names of fellow church members and friends. (She had covered up for him in conversations.) But what she hadn't realized was: Forgetfulness (to such a degree) is not a symptom of aging. It hadn't been old age. Ray was beginning the typical time clock of Alzheimer's.

In the beginning stages, victims can more competently conjure old memories of the past than the present news of the day. For instance, Ray had not been able to remember the morning's sermon yet he had been able to recount many times the sixty year old story about how his parents forbade him to learn piano....

A young boy sat writing at his old, oak desk; impatiently, his pencil forged across the page words that would come together to form his sixth grade research paper. The small scholar was Ray.

The paper should have been an easy assignment for the bright young boy. Had it not been for a distraction, he would have been finished. What was distracting him?

The room was plain. A bed, a navy rug, a lamp, and a desk. A tiny window overlooked the front of the farmhouse; not one thing in his room preoccupied his mind.

It was quiet—except for music echoing up from beneath the vibrating old floorboards. Piano music—his sole distraction.

His right hand gripped a pencil that dragged one last word onto the page. Fully surrendering to his diversion, Ray ceased writing. Longingly, he listened to Mildred practice.

Putting his pencil to the side, his hand was freed. The

boy closed his eyes as he sat with his head resting on his motionless left hand. His fingers mimicked the music and played upon an invisible piano. Suddenly, his right hand became not one that belonged to a wistful young farm boy but instead it became the hand of an accomplished pianist! As Mildred intolerantly forced herself to play "Take My Life and Let It Be," above her sat an eager Ray joyfully pretending to play. When the practice ended, so did Ray's fantasy. Reality hit him.

A frown crossed his childish face. Why couldn't he take piano lessons, anyway? Mildred and Alice were (at times) reluctant to take lessons; why did he have to just listen and pretend? He felt that he loved the piano much more than anyone in the family!

A few years before, Ray had pleaded with his parents to let him take piano lessons. They had said that he was too young.

Now he was older; he saw no reason why he would be prevented the privilege. Courage surged throughout his entire being as he pushed out the creaky desk chair with enthusiasm. He would ask his folks tonight!

Ray slowly peeked around the corner nearest the stairway. Berny sat cross-legged in his old rocker (he had made it maybe twenty years earlier) while reading the Omaha Herald. Ray felt his hands chill as he faced the obstacle of convincing his stubborn father. The newspaper rattled and Berny's eyes peeked over the pages and pierced Ray's face.

"Do you want something, son?"

Ray gulped. Stunned, he realized that he wasn't done with his homework! Because of that, he would never receive a chance— though he would receive a reprimand! In a state of near panic, Ray took flight and flew up the stairs like a cat-hunted bird.

Again, he worked on his haunting homework.

At the very moment of its completion, Ray headed down to his parents. He faced the forked road where to the right laid the *"town of piano lessons"* and to the left laid the *"city of absolutely not."* This time, he would get definite directions.

"Mom …. Dad, I've been wanting to ask you something." Mrs. Nellie Beamer knitted in a chair situated adjacent to Dad—still in his old rocker. Nellie pointed at a chair with her red yarn-wrapped knitting needles. Dad put his papers down next to him where they rustled onto the multicolored rug that hugged the old wood floor. Ray took a seat where the needles commanded. He gripped the smooth oak armrests with the intensity of a desperate man hanging onto a cliff where a mere wrong approach would lead to a deadening fall.

"I was just wondering if I could take piano lessons. I really enjoy listening to the piano and I'd sure love to learn how to play," Ray pleaded as he slid his shoes underneath his chair giving an utmost uncomfortable front. It was a full demonstration of his nervous mental state.

"Well, Ray, money is tighter these days." She appeared puzzled upon how to handle her "atypical" son. Her burgundy flowered dress draped around her gave her a dignified, beautiful appearance.

"But besides that, girls are better piano players than boys. It would be more fitting if we invested the money in something more suitable—like maybe a hunting gun. Many boys your age wish that they could hunt for their families," Mom answered. Though she rationalized her position, it was, in this case, totally irrational. As soon as Ray heard her intolerant tone of voice and observed her patronizing face, he realized that the acquisition was doomed.

"Your mother's right, son. You're almost twelve. Maybe someday we can look into getting a gun for you. And besides, piano playing doesn't bring food onto the table." His dad had to agree with Nellie. It was no secret that they were treading turbulent waters that day.

The verdict was in. Ray felt like he was a condemned convict being judged for his conflicting personality; he didn't fit into their mold. Suddenly, his armchair was transformed into an electric chair. His chance at piano lessons was electrocuted to death. Only his undying wish survived. He left the room in silence and trudged upstairs to go to bed. As he was midway up the stairs he heard his mother say:

"Sometimes, I just don't understand that boy."

Ray thought to himself as he wiped a tear from his face: "Sometimes, I don't understand you."

Chapter Eight
THE BOY HAS POLIO

Unintentionally, Ruth's grandparents had hurt her dad so severely that even with dementia, he hadn't forgotten his painful childhood. At least her dad had been able to talk a lot about his feelings concerning his piano lessons' rebuke. At least he had been able to talk about how he had felt when he listened to his sisters play the piano day after day, month upon month for years until he went to teachers' college. At least he could speak about it with his family. But as Ruth sat in the living room, she discovered how little he had shared over the years about his tragic bout with an extremely serious disease.

He had been a very young child. Ray had contracted and lived through another horrifying disease besides Alzheimer's. An illness that had physically crippled him. An illness that had caused him to limp even as an eighty-six year old man. He had suffered from a disease that affected his body almost as much as Alzheimer's had afflicted his mind. Poliomyelitis—better known as polio.

The virus usually enters the alimentary tract and spreads along nerve cells to affect sections of the nervous system. Because nerve cells that control muscular movement aren't replenished once they are destroyed, poliovirus infection can cause permanent paralysis. When nerve cells in the respiratory centers (which control breathing) are destroyed, the victim must be kept alive by an iron lung. It can lead to deformities. It can lead to fatalities.

Early symptoms include fatigue, headache, fever, vomiting, constipation, stiffness of the neck, and/or (though less frequent) diarrhea and pain in the extremities.... This exact disease, with all of its terror, is exactly what little, five year old Ray Beamer was suffering from and fighting with in the year of 1917 ....

"Berny! Ray's in bed with a high fever." Nellie declared at the bottom of the staircase. She gripped her apron in her writhing hands as she, with distraught eyes, looked into the living room where her husband sat in his old rocker. She was the total and complete example of a worry-crazed mother.

Berny put his papers down with one mighty, bear-like swipe of his hand. He stood up with one swift movement. He stared into his wife's eyes which were dancing with fear.

"Should we call the doctor?" Nellie quivered. Berny raised his eyebrows so that they climbed one quarter of the height of his high forehead. With eyebrows in position, Berny enunciated his words:

"He's *that* sick?!" He took his mighty hand and used it to rub across the length of his long face and looked away.

"I'm...afraid so," Nellie fretted.

He gripped his slightly pointed chin as he made one of the wisest announcements of his life:

"I'll go get the doctor." As he spoke, he gave his wife's shaking hand a quick squeeze.

"I'll...try...to harness the fever while you're gone...." Nellie managed to keep her head even as her heart hurt.

By the time Nellie was at the top of the stairs, Berny was out the door. By the time Nellie was at her small son's side, Berny was situated atop his horse. By the time Ray realized how sick he felt, Nellie and Berny (though separated) simultaneously realized how much they loved their endangered son.

"Mama, will I be okay?" Ray earnestly asked. His large eyes were a concoction of illness, fear, and innocence only a small boy could display.

Nellie pushed an off-white rag into a wooden bowl full of cool water. The water splattered as she squeezed the excess back into the bowl.

"If the Lord allows," Nellie answered with a distant stare as she stroked his hot head with the cooling cloth.

"Your father is getting the doctor."

"What are Mildred and Alice doing?"

"Well, Alice is playing the piano and Mildred is playing with dolls."

Ray sat up with a startled expression.

"Is she playing with one of my dolls you made for me?" he asked with childish worry.

"I don't know, but I have to get another cloth for you and while I'm downstairs I'll check."

"Thank you, Mama," Ray said with a gentle smile as he reclined back. His mama was kind.

A few minutes later, Nellie resumed the tender care of her son. She sat down on his little bed and tried her best to comfort, console, and care for her little boy.

Since Alice was the oldest, Nellie had trusted her to watch Mildred. Alice usually kept Mildred under good control, however, since she had been practicing her music, she had let down her guard. Because of the neglecting to watch her little sister, a disheartening happening occurred: Accidently, Mildred broke Ray's farmer doll.

Nellie knew how much her son loved his dolls; she had to break it to him as softly as possible—but, how?

How could she tell her dangerously ill son, that his all-time favorite toy was halved in two? The answer became evident when Ray turned to his worn-out mother and asked:

"Is my farmer doll okay? Could I have it in bed with me?"

Nellie took her son's small, pale hand and held it between hers. She swallowed hard.

"Son, this has not been a good day for either of us: You are very sick. I regret having to tell you this—but right is right and I must be completely honest with you. Mildred *was* playing with your doll and while Alice was playing the piano, Mildred broke it. I looked it over and I just can't fix it."

With every word she spoke, Ray's face paled and with her final statement, his watery, feverish eyes filled and flowed like waterfalls. (A few weeks earlier, he had buried one of his dolls so that his sisters wouldn't find them. The face had come off in the dirt and now his remaining doll was broken.) Nellie wiped away his tears and tried to think of something to say.

"Now, now, now, Ray. You are five years old. You are a little older to be playing with dolls anyway.... Oh! I think I hear the doctor. I'll go bring him up." Nellie regretted not being able to comfort her child but the doctor's care was more important than the doleful console.

Nellie had been correct about the doctor's arrival. She greeted the doctor with the same worry-stricken expression as she had given her husband. Taking the oil lamp, she led the doctor and her husband up the staircase. With its shadowy light, they entered the small room which housed the small boy.

"Well, now, Ray. Let me take a look at you," Doc Brenner greeted as he set his big brown bag onto the floor next to Ray's desk with a thump.

Doc Brenner was a large, intimidating man to the small, impressionable boy. Red caterpillars crawled above his eyes with the least likening to eyebrows. His eyes were close together and his nostrils far apart. Below his large Roman nose hung a fiery red mustache. The old, gray suit was pulled tautly around his round, rolling trunk.

Doc Brenner thudded across the old, loosening, wood floor and surveyed his patient. Ray's large, blue eyes were dull with fever. His little frame barely created a lump in the pile of covers; only his ashen, timid visage peeked out from beneath the heavy blankets. The rag that hung upon his forehead was warm from his fever. His face was soaked with sweat and tears. He was a very sick little soul.

Doc pulled out Ray's desk chair and creaked it over to the bed's side. Ray was scared but he was too sick to put up a fight. He was having trouble fighting the fever let alone a big, brawny man; he allowed the doctor to do whatever he wanted.

The prognosis was terrible. Following the examination, Doc Brenner covered the boy up to his chin and wished him a sober farewell. He once again followed Nellie's light and went down the stairway. When the tense threesome stood at the bottom of the stairs, Doc Brenner looked into Berny's eyes and then down at Nellie's.

"Could we speak in the living room?" Doc Brenner's deep voice echoed into the kitchen where Alice sweetly held Mildred. All inhabitants held their breath. The somber group, as a funeral march, headed into the living room.

Nellie's small frame sat near Berny's on the small sofa. Doc Brenner plopped onto Berny's big rocker. Only the crackling fire in the fireplace made the slightest sound. Then Doc's booming voice began the stomach churning conversation.

"Mr. and Mrs. Beamer," he paused for the words he would speak were terrifying. Terrifying to the boy, terrifying to the parents, and terrifying to the community. Suspense hung in the room like the deepest, darkest thunderclouds about to release their fury. Finally, he continued.

"Mr. and Mrs. Beamer," he repeated fully noticing Nellie's frantic squeeze of Berny's hand.

"The boy has polio."

Nellie cried in a hoarse, horrified whisper as she, with great urgency, clasped her hand across her open mouth: "*No!!!*"

Chapter Nine
NEITHER WOMAN FOUND THE ANSWERS

"Do you have any doubts, Doc?" Berny was grasping for any oversight only to find himself empty-handed. "I'm sorry. If I had doubts, I would be apprehensive but his is a classic case."

Berny tenderly wrapped an arm around Nellie almost as though he were trying to pick up the pieces of his shattered wife.

"I know that having your boy sick is hard enough-you understand the position I'm in—but I'm forced to quarantine your farm until Ray is well or...."

"We understand," Berny, took a big breath, and replied as he distantly stared down at the floor....

Days tediously turned their course as the bedridden Ray barely survived. The rambunctious, lively little boy now was a lethargic, dwindling child. No one but Nellie tended to his needs. Polio was not only deadly, it was contagious and the young Beamer parents desperately tried to protect the other children. She appeared almost as worn as Ray. Day after day, night after night, Nellie carried cool cloths to her son. Day after day, night after night, family members prayed for her son. Their prayers were answered on the seventh day of the fever: the fever broke and he was alive.

The fever was dead but people's prejudice of polio was alive and well; it left Ray with few friends. People talked; people stayed away. There were many misconceptions about the viral disease. Even though they could understand the dreadful fear of polio, Berny and Nellie still felt indignant toward tasteless gossips and the rumors with which they flowed. They were a clean family with high moral standards yet the rumors portrayed otherwise....

In fact, the same friends, with whom they had brushed elbows at church, would drive sections away just to avoid their farm. When Berny would look out through the kitchen screen door, he saw no one's buggy except their own. At the most, he would see dust a mile away. In this case, ignorance was not bliss—it was pernicious. It was vicious. After a few weeks, Ray steadily recovered. With each passing day, Ray became a bit more strong and rosy-cheeked. Little Ray didn't seem to understand why people had deserted him. Praise God, he couldn't comprehend the nature of their withdrawal.

Ray had been absent from church for seven straight Sundays. The Beamer family was a church-going family and as soon as it was feasible, Ray found himself in his Sunday attire sitting in the back of the black buggy. When they finally pulled into their old parking spot, people were staring. No one would have guessed when he peeked out and smiled that he had fought polio. Yet when Berny lifted little Ray up and out of the buggy, people turned their heads and the full factuality of his disease was confirmed.

Berny encompassed his small son's hand and Nellie held the other. Mildred and Alice stayed close behind. They all were a sight to see.

Berny wore his best Sunday black suit and his hair was slicked into place. Nellie wore her hair swept into a bun with a purple dress trailing below. Bobbing along in her fluffy little purple dress, tiny, curly brown-haired Mildred was followed closely by Alice as she stepped alongside in her blue flowered ensemble.

And then, there was Ray. His little black suit jacket edged up against his black knickers and his black knickers fell

Aunt Ruth was such a blessing! She truly was and is such a treasure whom we love and cherish. She always livened up Papa's Alzheimer's darkened world. Don't they look like they are enjoying themselves?! The farm visit was a true success! Here, they are shown visiting a friend's farm. Papa (having grown up on a farm) enjoyed it so much! He happily held baby goats and lambs. However, one can see the change in his eyes. Alzheimer's disease caused his sparkling blue eyes to become dull.

against his knees. His deformed knee and leg stood out like twisted, gnarled wood on a pile of straight planks. Between his gliding parents, the brave, limping young boy didn't quite "fit in" anymore.

As the family trekked along toward the church door, people smiled at cute little Mildred, they admired Nellie's dress, and they envied Alice's beautiful hair. But when they turned and saw Ray, they drew in a quick breath. Grins would turn into grimaces and Ray sensed that he had turned into a shunned spectacle rather than a normal boy. Mrs. Potts, his sisters' piano teacher whom he really liked, was the only sincere, loving Christian who came up to Ray and gave him a big hug. Others, trying to be polite, would tell them how sorry they were— although their faces displayed their distaste.

By the time the entire church experience was over, Ray felt as though God wouldn't like the way the people had acted. Ironically, the minister had preached upon how Christ had loved and healed a cripple.

Ray felt like a cripple being shunned by the Pharisees. Hypocrites had shunned cripples while Christ had welcomed them with open, loving, healing arms.

Later that day, Nellie sat down in her rocker and mulled over the entire experience. She had been well aware of the stares, the hidden mockery, and the general air of unease. Then, she asked a question that she would continue to ponder for many years: "Why did polio have to attack my boy?"

Seventy years later, the same "boy" was suffering from another disease; Ruth had to ask a very similar question as she sat in her chair:

"Why did Alzheimer's have to attack my dad?"

Neither women ever found the answers.

Chapter Ten
CHRISTMAS AND ALZHEIMER'S

Just like their lives, two days after Ruth had painstakingly put their old tree together, it had crashed down and collapsed in a heap of silver garland, multicolored lights, sparkling tinsel, antique ornaments, and a shining star. Just like Ray, the outward parts were still there but it was not the same.

When the tree was repositioned, it had a fraction of the majesty it once had exhibited. It was slanted and the branches were crooked. Occasionally, a scrap of garland would fall upon the lonely gifts that laid strewn across the tree skirt.

The few presents that existed had been quickly wrapped by a depleted Ruth. No gifts were joyfully purchased, carefully wrapped, and lovingly placed under the tree by Ray and Hilda—the Christmas couple.

Not so long ago, Ray and Hilda would have shopped for their kids, grandkids, friends, and neighbors. They were a couple of Christians that truly loved Christmas. Not a single person could deny that they had exhibited great love.

Every year at Christmas time, Ray and Hilda shopped in Le Mars and then headed to Sioux City where stores were graced by their love and gleeful faces. Clerks loved to serve them. Managers loved their personalities as much as their money. Toy stores expected them as birthdays expect a cake. Everyone loved Ray and Hilda and Ray and Hilda loved it all.

But, no Ray and Hilda were to be seen in the corridors of the cities' stores this season. Clerks missed their presence. Managers missed their friends more than the couple's money. And toy stores were missing two special patrons. The birthday was without the cake.

Instead, the two casualties of Alzheimer's now sat at home where the sick Christmas tree loomed in the living room.

Ruth was the only reserve left to shop for the family. Now, it was vice versa. Ruth shopped for Ray and Hilda.

Even though Ray's affliction prevented them from all-out shopping, decorating, baking, and going to Christmas church functions, one tradition remained unchanged: the Stoelting's would come to celebrate....

The Beamer's weren't the only ones looking forward to the gift exchange. Carrie and Stacie counted the days until they would be able to celebrate Christmas at Papa and Grandma's house. When Christmas Eve finally showed its face, Carrie and Stacie greeted it with wide, anticipating smiles.

The granddaughters were well prepared. Because the girls had limited finances, they patronized the dollar store. For months in advance, they would shop for the perfect gifts and now it was *the* day! As they waited to leave, Stacie and Carrie held the gifts which, to them and their recipients, were treasures.

They now stood in the foyer, patiently waiting for their departure. Wendell was downstairs stocking his video camera's case with supplies for a full day of taping. He was (as always) dressed and ready; his reddish brown hair was properly combed and his tall frame wore a navy blazer and tan pants. (He was wearing new glasses and the family had yet to notice!) Mary was still getting dressed in her sparkling holiday attire—but she wasn't the only Stoelting trying to look festive. Stacie and Carrie wore socks with jingling bells, blouses with holiday flares, and their hair and shoes were adorned with silly red bow decorations. They may have looked silly, but they were having so much fun!

Hilda and Ruth tried their ultimate best to clean up for the Christmas celebration. Hilda wore a flowered blouse with black slacks, Ray sat in a blue sweat outfit, and Ruth wore her Christmas tree sweatshirt. Ruth gleefully placed some Christmas candy inside Carrie's and Stacie's stockings. Both caregivers prayed that Ray would remain clean when the guests arrived.

When it was 2:00 PM, the navy Lincoln Town Car pulled up next to the walkway. Almost unable to get to the door without collapsing, the four Stoelting's were glad to lay down their huge boxes of gifts near the door. Their breath became a white vapor as they stood at the doorway. Did anyone greet them?

Of course! From the moment they had pulled up, Hilda's sparking eyes had watched their every move! If she had been steadier on her feet,

Left to Right: Stacie, Mary, and Carrie. Merry Christmas! For Christmas, our (loved-like-a-relative) neighbor, Sandy Specht, handmade these cute, coordinating Christmas sweatshirts; we had fun wearing holiday attire to Papa and Grandma's house.

she would have been helping them unload. But ice and old age just don't mix! Yes—they were greeted; by two enthusiastic greeters, Hilda and Ruth!

"It's so great to see you, Mom!" Mary exclaimed as her arms opened wide to surround Hilda with love.

Then, came the girls. They took turns eagerly greeting Grandma and Aunt Ruth with sincere affection. Where was Wendell? Had he been forgotten during this display? Surely not! As soon as he jovially smiled and said, "Hi,

Hilda!" she gently gave him a hug and a peck on his beaming face.

From the moment the first visitors stepped over the threshold, Hilda and Ruth shrouded them with hugs and kisses. All four shifted to and fro as they took their turns. Usually, Hilda would give them the first love-filled session and then Ruth would give them her love round. Not too long ago, there would have been three rounds of love expressions. But it was not so anymore. Instead, the happy, joy-filled greetings were solemnly silenced as they respectfully, reverently proceeded into the den where Ray (in his chair) sat with his arms crossed.

Everyone sort of huddled insecurely shadowing the entrance to the room; after all, they weren't aware of his mood. Slowly, but lovingly, Mary tested the waters.

"Hi, Daddy," she soothed as she slowly stepped over and tenderly held his hand.

"Hi," Ray's voice wavered. Still, though in his horrid state of health, he showed his love to his family; for with her hand in his, he slowly brought it to his lips and kissed it. He smiled up at her and then to the rest of the now-relaxing clan.

"I'm... glad you're here."

"We are, too!" Stacie exclaimed as she bent down and kissed his forehead while he sweetly kissed her hand.

Following the cease of the general sense of ill ease, the family was greatly relieved to find Ray in such good spirits—considering his bad state.

Following the entire family's acknowledgment of their failing family member, they gradually positioned themselves in the Christmas main station: the living room.

At the front of the long room with the vaulted ceiling sat the Nativity scene—the reminder of the center of the family's celebration. To the left of it hung Ruth's large, gold, chandelier-like decoration in the doorway. To the right of the Nativity stood the once mighty tree, propped near the large window with the stained glass top.

Like traditional years of past, the family discussed and visited about life. Like an almost instituted ritual, Carrie and Stacie searched and panned over the tree skirt for the presents denoted with their names. All trials and pestilences could not take away the love engraved on their hearts.

As soon as the ladies finished the last touches to the meal, the men and children would await their calling.

Ray and Wendell couldn't have the complicated, pal-like discussions they once shared, but they still could talk a little and watch a little television while they waited. After all, they still shared an interest in watching a good game.

"Wow! That was a good play!" Wendell exclaimed as he turned the lever on the rust-colored recliner. It pulled out the foot rest, which had a spring that creaked.

"Yeah," Ray agreed as he tapped his treasured ruby ring (given by his very close friend, Hilda's mother) on the wooden part of the armrest. He sat in the twin of Wendell's old recliner.

Stacie and Carrie were playing with the cat, Cutie. He just loved string! They would lead him from one end of the living room to the next. Pretty soon, Cutie ran into the den and out into the kitchen. He had heard Aunt Ruth open the cat food.

As Cutie scampered through the den and past the two sport watchers, everyone had a comical reminder of Ray's disease.

"There goes the horse!" Ray exclaimed. This time, it was better to laugh than to cry.

Suddenly, Hilda rounded the corner. She made a funny, snooty face by putting her nose into the air like a snobby butler. Then with a voice to match her face, she made the announcement that all had been waiting for: "Dinner is served!"

Stacie and Carrie had to keep themselves from running and zealously fell into the chairs which were next to their grandma's. They always felt special sitting next to her! Across from Carrie, Hilda, and Stacie sat two of the three chefs.

Mary was seated next to Wendell's unoccupied chair and was directly across from Hilda. Ruth (at Mary's left side) sat directly across from Stacie; she appeared to barely refrain from eating. Her eyes seemed to eye the food with increased impatience and fervor. She looked over at Stacie and smacked her lips in anticipation. Mary softly laughed at her sister. It seemed like whenever she was hungry, she was starved! Hilda was well aware of her daughter's hunger. She looked at Mary and gave a fitting remark with one of Hilda's cherished smiles:

"You'd think we never feed her!"

All the girls laughed in unison. Ever since Alzheimer's, Hilda had made a tremendous effort to still act happy when the granddaughters were there; she never wanted Alzheimer's to destroy their special bond.

Then everyone held their breath; Ray slowly lumbered into the room with hair astray, clothes rumpled. Everyone was seated except for Ray and Wendell. He looked bewildered. Not knowing where he should be seated, he grimaced. Then, he headed toward Wendell's still vacant chair.

"No, Ray. You get to sit here," Wendell explained and offered as he pulled out the chair which had undoubtedly been Ray's for many years. Ray looked into Wendell's gray eyes and looked down as though he sensed that something was wrong with him. He regained the small fraction of what at one time was his composure, and forged his way back to where Wendell still stood. He then, with a sigh, took his place at the head of the dining room table. Immediately, Mary gently straightened his hair and gave him a little kiss on his forehead. Still upset, Ray barely managed to say "thank you."

In years past, the table would have been in a buzz with all of the talk and laughter, but not this year. Everyone was walking on eggshells. Ray's mood was a tad shaky. His face seemed disturbed ever since he had felt a very faint realization of a faulty mentality. Wendell felt he had to do something to leaven the mood.

"I'll be right back," Wendell said as he headed toward the living room.

"But we're ready to eat, what are you doing?" Mary said ever so slightly aggravated.

"I'm going to get the video camera. You three prepared such a wonderful meal, I think it needs to be recorded." Pretty soon he appeared grinning from ear to ear as he propped the heavy, large object onto his shoulder. Mary shook her head with a faint smile. He and she had disagreed many times over how much he should record and on how necessary it was to use the large camera when there were hand-held video recorders on the market.

"Today is December 24, 1998—Christmas Eve at Hilda and Ray's. We are about to have a wonderful meal that was prepared by Mary, Hilda, and Ruth. It looks wonderful!" Wendell said as his stomach rumbled. He had a mischievous satisfaction when he focused upon Mary's half-smiling, barely tolerant face.

"Don't you think you could put it down. We are all *hungry*," Mary enunciated as she looked into the camera.

Wendell panned the table once more: Mary's honey and pineapple ham, Mary's white, fluffy, warm rolls with butter and jelly, Grandma's homemade mashed potatoes, Hilda's cherry Jell-O fruit salad, all-famous potato salad and "Stacie Salad" (a salad which was named in honor of one of its most dedicated admirers), and Ruth's fantastic cornbread with green bean casserole nearby. Wendell finally turned the camera off and settled down into his place.

"Papa Ray, would you say the prayer?"

Stacie had asked so sweetly that no one had the heart to tell her. It wasn't feasible since he had failed. All of the adults looked at each other uneasily, even sadly. Because no one had replied, Stacie tried again.

"Papa, could you say the prayer?"

Before Mary could finally speak, something stopped her. Ray's voice slowly began the touching prayer he had offered so many times to our Heavenly Father.

"Heavenly Father, we thank You for the food which Thou hast provided for us. Bless it to the nourishment of our bodies. Forgive us of our sins. We ask it all in Thy Name. Amen."

It was a gift from God. Everyone felt a special, tremendous sensation. God never forsook them. God's presence filled the room and their grateful hearts...

After a full feast, the family's stomachs were offered a top off for the meal: Mary's sugar cookies and cherry pie. (Ray always adored cherry pie.) Mary had helped contribute so as to lighten the already overloaded Hilda and Ruth. When the two girls were done with dessert, they knew it was almost time....

Then it came; one of the most anticipated moments of all: the gift exchange.

"Oohs" and "ahs" circulated throughout the room and resonated in the excitement. Discarded wrappings were as numerous as the exclamatory words spoken. All laps were decorated with presents. The room, which most of the time felt painfully empty, now was brimming with companionship, love, happiness, and gifts.

Though the presents were bought by human beings, the gifts were actually from God; the One Who inspired them to purchase the presents. Though the love was expressed by human beings, it actually was from God; the One Who inspired them to express good, clean-cut affection.

Every year Carrie and Stacie would observe (with tremendous exuberance) the custom of having extremely special gifts usually hand-given by Ray and Hilda. The "surprise" gifts were parceled out only after all other gifts were exposed.

One year, they were ruby red bean bag chairs, another year they were a race car mountain and doll hair salon, another year it was a rocking horse, and this year, well, it certainly was a surprise!

When the rest of the giving was done and the "oohs"

and "ahs" were silenced, Stacie and Carrie grinned. They exchanged anxious glances as they awaited the special "surprise."

Knowingly, Hilda smiled and giggled softly. She slowly arose and stole away to her hiding spot. Then, with overflowing glee, she handed over two 20" by 10" boxes which were lovingly wrapped in comic newspaper. Hands flew and soon two white, smooth boxes emerged. Stacie knew what it was; it was the gift she had wanted for years! Carrie had an idea, but she was too excited to guess. Almost simultaneously, two American Girl dolls opened their glass eyes for the first time. Stacie's arms encircled "Samantha" and Carrie clung to "Kirsten." Then, with exclamatory yelps and shocked gasps the two overjoyed children rushed over and gave their Papa Ray and Grandma Hilda kisses and hugs. This time, the girls' excitement was not overshadowed by Alzheimer's. Papa Ray even seemed to enjoy the general feeling of joyful commotion. He still had the inkling to play with dolls and he made Samantha and Kirsten dance on his armrest. Papa Ray and the grandchildren laughed in delight. But they never would spend another Christmas like that one, again....

Chapter Eleven
THAT WAS NOT HER DAD!

Months went by as slowly as any others in the Beamer household; the only difference was the undeniable fact that Ray's condition had severely worsened. Ray had failed enough that he couldn't even attend Stacie's party in the spring.

When Stacie had her birthday party, Papa wasn't there to make her laugh, blow the noise blower in people's faces, or open her gifts with his old, trusty pocket knife. Stacie had tried to enjoy the party but it wasn't the same. After everyone had gone home, reality had fallen upon her that he wouldn't come to her parties anymore. She fled into her parents' bedroom and cried.

Yes, he had touched many lives and as he regressed, his life, like a rock causing ripples in a pond, left numerous, widespread hearts' aching for his presence.

Ruth worked in the garden once tilled by the man with the old denim jacket. Katy and Hilda chatted but Mert missed conversing with his good old friend. Carrie and Stacie played with the American Girl dolls and loved talking to Grandma and Aunt Ruth—though they truly missed their relationship with the real Papa Ray. When Wendell had a problem, he couldn't ask his old pal for legitimate advice. Mary and Ruth missed their old problem—lifting Daddy. Hilda's heart ached for her old romantic Ray. When Lawrence came back in the early summer, he missed his old talks with the man whom he so respected.

Besides the family's heartache, some happy moments had appeared floating in the distance upon their sea of sadness: Lawrence arrived.

Flying all of the distance from Texas, much effort was exerted by the family friend. Much effort was exerted by the family as well. It might as well have been a holiday! His arrival meant a delicious dinner in the best restaurant in town, a wonderful visit, and countless hugs. His arrival also presented a problem. What would they do with Ray?

Due to his deteriorated condition, the family (after much prayer and thought) decided to place Ray in respite; a lengthened form of adult daycare. The Alzheimer's Association helped to locate the best establishment in the area. Incredibly, Ray didn't seem to mind!

The entire family and their honored guest now enjoyed fantastic food, fellowship, and fun by being together at the best restaurant in town. The table was bombarded with the buzz of constant conversation. What were the plans for the future? How was life in Texas? How was Lawrence's job? How was his family? There were too many questions calling for responses!

Now, during what should have been a delightful dinner, Hilda felt despondent; she hid her feelings. She loved Lawrence very much. But she so loved Ray...and Ray wasn't there. She felt "as though her right arm had been cut off." Such a bond existed between them that even though it was a short time (with one spouse astoundingly afflicted), Hilda (and even Ray) missed one another tremendously. How could she enjoy the pile of food on her plate when her heart hurt so much? How could she possibly adjust to the vacant chair beside her? Everyone else seemed to be loving every moment—and their food. Here sat Hilda hurting every moment. As the swirl of conversations continued, she couldn't help but drift into daydreaming.... Hilda couldn't help but recall how they had hated being apart. Even years ago, after just being separated while he was at work, she had missed his presence! Hilda remembered one particular day which had been exemplary of their bond.

— ❋ —

Anyone that met the Beamer couple knew that they were not just an ordinary couple...they were extraordinary! As a middle-aged pair, they treated one another as though they were still engaged. (That was one of the secrets to their marriage.)

One day, a depressed couple, Mr. and Mrs. Samuel Sadings, dropped by with an ulterior motive. They were having marriage problems and Mrs. Sadings thought that if her husband picked up on a few pointers from their host and hostess, maybe their marriage, too, would be better. Mr. Sadings, meanwhile, hoped that Mrs. Sadings would elicit some tips from the couple. Therefore, the pair now sat in the living room of their role models' home.

Before Ray came home from work, Hilda enjoyed trying to cheer them up. Hilda had noticed the intolerance which existed between the company whom she now entertained. Food cheers people up so Hilda served them coffee and tasty cookies....

"Here, have another cookie," Hilda offered with a mother-like sincerity.

"Thank you, I think I will," the depressed lady conceded.

"Hilda, how do you and Ray keep the spark alive in your marriage after you've been married for years?" Mrs. Sadings asked as she plucked another peanut butter cookie off of the blue plate. Her face showed the indifference to her husband sitting across from her. She looked up into Hilda's face showing the unsatisfied soul dwelling within her.

"You know, we have always been so in love that I guess it's been easy. We've always had such good times together. We've had our troubles, too, of course. But in

"Honey," Grandma said to Papa. "We've been married five years —let's have our picture taken!" And so they did and this is the picture! Where are my aunt and my mom? They weren't even born! It was to be years before they had children.

answer to your question: Have faith in God. Never go to bed angry."

To this, well embellished Mrs. Sadings glared at Mr. Sadings' small, suit-clothed frame in the wing backed chair. Mr. Sadings, a narrow man in body and mind, shifted uncomfortably in his chair and cleared his throat under his plump wife's dark eyed stare.

"And…. and, treat your spouse as though you are still engaged," Hilda continued hesitating now and then to gather her words. She sensed the tension so she tried to relieve it with a distraction: "Would you like another cookie, Mr. Sadings? I think that you would, wouldn't you?"

Mr. Sadings, relieved to have a diversion, gratefully accepted as he eyed the plate being offered to him. His eyeglasses slid down his nose slightly as he looked down and he had to nudge them up before selecting his cookie. This, too, lent him an uneasy air.

"Thank you, Hilda." He took the cookie and smiled at her. Then, in a blink of an eye, he glanced over at Mrs. Sadings to find her frowning at him. He quickly gulped and looked down at the floor.

"Will we get to see Ray?" Mrs. Sadings inquired as she munched on her cookie. It was her sixth one. No wonder she was considerably overweight.

"Why, I think you will! He's coming up the walk!" Hilda said as she rushed to the door—almost forgetting about her company.

As soon as Ray entered the home, the stiff Sadings' were in for a shock. Ray abruptly dropped his briefcase, Hilda flew into his arms and she gave him quite a kiss! Looking into his eyes, she said lovingly, caringly, and so sincerely what she said every single day:

"This is my favorite part of the day, honey!"

"Mine, too, sweetheart," he whispered as he stroked her cheek gently. Was this a dream or did the Sadings' actually see what they thought they saw? Was it actually possible to be so in love without being hypocrites?

This is a couple married for fourteen years?! Mr. and Mrs. Samuel Sadings just looked at each other. The last time that they had loved one another so passionately was before their marriage—during their engagement. They had been married merely five years and already their relationship had soured. Meanwhile, Mr. and Mrs. Ray Beamer had grown more attached and their relationship had even sweetened! Unbelievable!

With a proud arm about her shoulder, Hilda and Ray greeted their guests once more.

"They truly do seem engaged," Mrs. Sadings thought to herself. She turned toward her husband and mouthed the word: *"See!"* Mr. Sadings attempted to shape his mouth into half of a smile and swallowed hard. How he envied Ray, Hilda, and their <u>unusual marriage</u>!

"Hi! How are you folks doing?" Ray cheerfully, caringly inquired.

Mr. Sadings' frown quickly subsided into a beaming smile.

"Everything's wonderful!" He beamed as he lied between his teeth. He unconsciously rubbed his nose as he spoke. No, it hadn't grown out like Pinnochio's. Only his reputation as a proud liar had grown.

Ray, knowing that the man had lied, prayed for a way to lead the poor person down God's path. Within a short prayer, he decided not to sound "preachy" and chose to say:

"You know, they say that behind every great man is a great woman…. So we must be great men!"

As he rolled his eyes and looked at Hilda he beamed and said simply: "Aren't we blessed?!"

Mr. Sadings just stared off into the distance. God was touching his heart….

— ❄ —

The memory grew foggy and Hilda could not remember any more of the visit. Besides, it was dessert time and everyone was talking about what kind of ice cream, cake, or pastry they were going to order.

"Grandma, what dessert are you going to have?" Carrie excitedly asked as she smiled broadly.

"What, honey?"

"What kind of dessert are you going to order?"

"I haven't been thinking about it, sweetie," Hilda said as she made herself a part of the celebration once more. She smiled slightly to accommodate her treasured granddaughter.

"What are you going to have, honey?" Ruth lovingly asked Lawrence—fully unaware of her choice of words.

Stacie whispered to Carrie:

"*Did you hear that? She called him HONEY!*" Both young girls giggled.

Soon thereafter, Lawrence and the family finished their meals. Soon thereafter, Lawrence returned to Texas but not without taking Ruth's love and concern with him.

No doubt lingered in anyone's mind about the fact that when Lawrence had come back, the romance had been rekindled. Ruth's face had radiated whenever he was even spoken of casually. Lawrence, though bubbling with happiness, remained cautiously optimistic about their courtship. Lawrence called more often than before—and Ruth certainly called him even more.

Following Lawrence's return to Texas, Mary gazed at the peach lace suit she once bought for Ruth's wedding mirage. This time, Mary was hopeful that maybe she would become a matron of honor after all; time would tell.

After Lawrence and Ruth's relationship had been revived, it had served as a catalyst for Hilda to start analyzing her daughter. Many a night, when she couldn't sleep, Hilda would think about her daughter whom she treasured so much. Hilda just trusted the Lord about her younger girl's future marital status. For Ray and she, trusting the Lord had always worked. They had truly relied heavily upon God when Hilda (in her forties) became expectant with Ruth Ann Beamer, their baby girl....

— ❄ —

Ray and Hilda surprised and even shocked the entire Nebraska small town. They were the gossip of the women's clubs, the talk of the men's coffee breaks. They stood on the center stage. Some agreed with them while others raised their eyebrows. What did a Christian couple do which would cause such petty turmoil and gossip?

Hilda was in her forties at the time, as was Ray. Ray and Hilda parented a pretty, blonde little five year old girl named Mary who enchanted all who met her. But Hilda and Ray were in their forties and no one had expected a miracle which would impose such gossip.

Hilda was expecting a baby in middle age.

In small town America, in the baby boomer era, it might as well have been a national shock! But, how did the awaiting couple feel about it? They were overjoyed! They hoped only that their baby would arrive safely and healthy. That was their main concern—not what the town thought of them.

It was an incredible time in their lives! How they had wanted the child! How they had wanted their little Mary to have a companion! Now, dreams were coming true....

"Hilda, you seem to be doing fine. The baby seems to be doing wonderfully! If any lady is youthful and could handle this, it's you!" Dr. Douglas Feshilist announced as he stood his full height of six feet and four inches following his examining her. If ever there was a specialist that knew how to protect both Hilda and the baby, it was Dr. D. Feshilist. Following that reasoning, Ray and Hilda had made him their doctor in the special time of their lives. No matter that they had to drive all the way into the big city. Ray himself had said that nothing was too good for his Hilda!

"I'm so thankful, Doctor! Every morning, noon, and night I pray that God will bless this baby. You haven't any idea how much we have dreamt of and anticipated this child," Hilda sincerely spoke her heart.

"By the look in your eyes, I think I can guess." Dr. Feshilist had seen many a parent and Hilda rated highly on his list. What a blessed child it would be if it arrived safely!

— ❋ —

Thank God, Ruth Ann Beamer had arrived safely. How blessed she was to have them as well as they were to have her!

— ❋ —

Time had passed; Mary and Wendell lived quite happily though they still gently disagreed about the camera. Lawrence and Ruth had parted completely; he remained a close friend of the family anyway. Ruth remained her pretty, fun-loving self; yet her dad was drifting deeper into the diseased fog. Pressure was mounting and it appeared that Ray didn't have much time at home. It was late July and Ray's condition was still worsening.

It was a warm night. Hilda sat in the dining room, unable to sleep. Hilda wasn't stupid. She knew that her Ray was failing. With a worried brow and a finger touching her mouth with concern, Hilda fought the idea. She fought the idea for she knew—wherever Ray was placed, he would die there. It chilled and shook her soul.

How could it be? Just a few months before he had been able to really enjoy the grandkids at Christmas, but now even they could not lift his fog. No more weeks existed during which Ray merely occasionally wandered. Now he roamed every night. He was becoming more violent.

Never during their fifty-six year old marriage had Ray been even remotely forceful. They had been a tender, well mannered, and fun-loving couple. During a section of her life when it should have been the "Golden Years" it had rusted into the "Copper Years." When she should have been fondly recalling pleasant milestones and memories with a happy heart, Hilda could barely start thinking about the old times because of the present panics.

One such obstacle tormented Hilda tremendously. Hilda couldn't help it as she replayed the nightmarish experience in her mind....

Lorraine Foley, their devoted friend and volunteer from the Alzheimer's Association, was coming over to act as a caregiver for Ray so that Hilda and Ruth could take what would prove to be a desolate break. They had planned to eat out with Mary and the girls but Ray's actions almost destroyed their plans.

Ruth had been taking care of a neighborly errand for their dear friend Mrs. Renken. Sadly, she had not been there when perhaps Hilda had needed her the most, if not only for moral support, but also for physical protection!

Shortly before Mary had pulled up, Ray went into a terrifying rampage. As Hilda tried to get his odious diaper off she had, in the process, been forced to take off his smelly, unfittingly dirty pajamas.

They had been in the small, cramped downstairs bathroom. He had been peaceful enough until a few moments after he had been stripped.

Then, for some unknown reason, something caused him to become entirely crazy.

He stomped wildly out of the restroom and plodded about the downstairs—without a stitch on! As the exhausted Hilda gaped in horror, she felt like she was almost in a dream—more like a horrible nightmare!

She walked into the den, then tried to coax him there so she could dress him.

"Here, Ray. Come here so that I can help you," Hilda was panting from the pathetic situation as she desperately tried to tell him to join her in the den. Her weak words of comfort were drowned out by the incessant obscenities as he paraded about the living room—dirtying Hilda's prized carpet, smearing feces upon the furniture and on the armrest on which he had once danced the American Girl dolls.

Prior to her coaxing, Hilda had still hoped that she would be able to successfully calm him. But after seeing that even *she* had no effect upon him, she became very frightened. What could she do? Would she have to call the police?

She stared powerlessly at him as he destroyed her living room with his filth. She just mouthed the name "Ray" because she was so heartsick that she couldn't speak.

If anyone had thought that it couldn't get any worse, they would have been wrong for suddenly, Ray turned toward Hilda.

The wild man turned and noticed her standing there alone. His eyes were wild like a prairie fire. He looked into his wife's eyes and yelled a sickening cuss word (a true manifestation of the disease).

"You ….!!!!!"

Hilda's soul felt deathly sick inside.

The naked, poop-covered old man (with hair flying) stomped swiftly into the den and headed straight for Hilda. As he plodded past Hilda, his left hand grabbed her right arm tightly and shoved the eighty-four year old lady onto the sofa so that she fell hard.

Hilda slumped to her side and prayed: "Dear Jesus, please, please help me!"

Only then, the God-send, Lorraine walked into the house. "Hilda! Are you all right?" Lorraine said as the pretty, pink-blouse-clothed lady with larger glasses rushed into the den.

"I'll be just fine," a weak, near weeping voice replied as she rubbed her stinging, red, injured arm. Lorraine, a retired nurse, felt her arm to be sure that it wasn't broken. Thank God, it would only be bruised.

"Where is Ray?" Lorraine asked but Hilda didn't have to answer her: for there came Ray rampaging around the corner. Ray kept going and seemed to head toward the living room.

Lorraine intersected his path as he headed through the room.

"Come on now, Ray! People love you and want to take care of you!" Lorraine consoled. Ray looked at her and took upon himself the mentality of an animal. He raised his fist and prepared to strike her. With the strength of a young man, he hit her arm with his left fist and smeared poop on her pretty pink blouse. Just then Mary walked into the front door.

As she walked in, expecting to be greeted with a hug by her mother, Mary was "greeted" by her father as he plodded past the door.

For the first time in her life, she saw her father naked, dung adorned, and completely, uncontrollably crazy. She stood there with a feeling of pure nausea and in her eyes tears formed.

This was not her dad!

Chapter Twelve
IT WAS TIME...

Hilda couldn't bear to remember and replay it anymore. Being a truly positive lady, she decided to find something else she could do that could take her mind off of her heart wrenching, almost crushing problems. She decided to catch up on her diary.

Paging through her green encased treasure, she scanned over the pages until she discovered a certain, invaluable entry. It was the day when Ray had saved Wendell's life. Yes, although it had been years, Hilda could remember the day as though it had been only yesterday; this memory was intense but something about it made her feel a swell of pride over her husband. What a hero.....

Mary and Wendell had been staying with Ray and Hilda ever since their house had become uninhabitable due to remodeling. (In fact, Ray had been the one to advise them about the remodeling.) They never had wanted to impose, but Ray and Hilda had welcomed them with open arms.

At the time that a certain incident occurred, the young married couple had been with the old married couple for about five months. And my, it had been a wonderful five months! They loved their times together: the visiting, the meals, the overall feeling of a fun time. And, after two years of marriage, Wendell and Mary were expecting their firstborn child. Things seemed to be almost perfect but there were, however, a few heavy hardships.

One difficulty existed due to the fact that Wendell was an optometrist in Cherokee; everyday he had to make a forty-five minute commute. Another much more serious, life threatening difficulty was the fact that Wendell was developing asthma. Severe asthma....

Daddy and Mama—They are such wonderful folks! In this picture, they had been married one year. (Papa walked her down the aisle, I might add!) Here, she is pregnant with me! Shortly after this photo was taken, they stayed with Papa and Grandma. Aren't they a happy looking young couple?! Note: Daddy was beginning to get sick ....

"Thanks, Hilda," Wendell said as she poured him some juice.

"You really didn't have to do this," he added earnestly as he looked gratefully up at Hilda's smiling face. Hilda had arisen early so that she could fix him some breakfast. When Wendell had come downstairs, Hilda had been ready with orange juice, cereal, pancakes, and fruit.

"But I wanted to," Hilda smiled then immediately frowned in intense concern; she could hear his lungs wheeze.

"Honey, do you have to go to work. You really are sick!"

"I'll be all right. But you know, I actually would stay home but with competition in town, I feel like I have to really keep my head up," he continued. He furrowed his brow in worry as he sipped the last of his orange juice. (He truly had a deep dedication to his patients; people appreciated his sincerity and detailed exams.)

"It's 7:00! I've got to go! Thanks again. Send my love to Mary. She had a poor night."

"Sure, but please come home if it's too much for you!" Hilda called after him. She prayed.

Not too long after Wendell departed, a yawning Ray entered the kitchen to find Hilda seated (with her head in her left hand) and no Wendell.

"Ah, shucks! I guess I missed him again!" Ray laughed. He never seemed to get up in time. But the foursome had been keeping late nights watching movies so it was a real effort to get up early.

"Yes," Hilda replied as she stared into the distance. Ray could sense that something was troubling his precious wife.

"Hilda. What's wrong? Is Wendell all right?!" Ray inquired with great urgency as he put his hand upon her shoulder. Hilda reached up and held his hand.

"He coughed terribly in the night and this morning. His cough is vicious! And…he was wheezing badly. I think he's getting worse. I'm worried about him, Ray."

"I am, too, honey," he replied as he joined Hilda in her concern. Now Ray joined Hilda as they both stared into the distance. Both issued a prayer for their beloved son in law….

It was 6:45 PM; Ray, Hilda, and an expectant Mary were well aware of Wendell's tardiness. They sat in the sun porch, fists tight, prayers said, and worrisome looks given. As the sun began to go down, it darkened not only the outdoors, it darkened their hopes as well.

Mary sat in a tan chair, illuminated by the dusky light. Hilda sat on the sofa next to Ray, nervously holding hands.

At last the old red car slowly pulled near the curb adjacent to the porch. Its advancement was well watched.

Ray ran to the door and opened it wide. There stood Wendell, pale as a walking corpse, gray as the dullest clouds. He heard him say a distant, weak whisper. Ray could barely make it out.

"*I...need...help!*" Wendell managed to say between weak breaths. He leaned against the door, almost collapsing. His breath intake seemed about a fiftieth of his lung capacity. He was barely alive.

"Hilda! Watch him while I go get the car. I'm taking this boy to the hospital!" Ray yelled as he ran as fast as possible to the garage. Hilda then tried to keep Wendell calm; she maintained control knowing that if he became excited, his breathing rate would be unable to sustain his life.

Then, faster than anyone could imagine, Ray had the white car pulled out. The seventy-one year old ran up the sidewalk and met Wendell at the door.

"Now, Mary, you carefully get into the car. Wendell, you lean on Hilda's and my shoulders," Ray commanded knowing the seriousness of the situation. Slowly, the youthful senior citizens took Wendell and helped him into the car. There Mary (by then) sat— expectant and very worried. She couldn't help but wonder:

"Would her child have a daddy?"

Meanwhile, Ray remained cool and collected, though inside, scared for his "adopted" son. He turned on the ignition and began the race against time and death.

He sped through the town and pulled out onto the highway. By then, Wendell's breath became a one second inhale and a one second exhale. Hilda stroked his cold cheek with her hand.

"Could you go any faster, Ray?!" she pleaded.

"I'll try!" Ray called to the back seat. He pushed the pedal to the floor.

Ray passed cars and hit speeds he never would have hit otherwise. He just prayed that the police wouldn't detain him. He wasn't sure Wendell would make it.

Finally, after what seemed like a three hour drive, Ray pulled the car to a halt. Ray flew out of the car and swung open Wendell's door. He reached in and helped Wendell out and into the hospital's emergency room using the same leaning technique.

The room was a buzz with activity and in their stressed out state, it seemed like no one was going to help him! Ray once again took control of the situation as a nurse walked by. Ray commanded the nurse with an authoritative voice: "Get this man help!!"

— ❄ —

The doctors worked and worked on him. They even said that had Ray not taken such action, Wendell would have died.

While he was being cared for, the prayerful three held their vigil in the waiting area. When no one else knew what to say, Ray turned to Hilda and Mary and said the pertinent statement Mary would never forget: "You know, I love that boy."

— ❄ —

Praise God, because of Ray, Wendell lived.

— ❄ —

Hilda had been so proud of her husband. He had proven to be such a wonderful man over the many years they had shared together. The time when he saved Wendell's life was not the only time that he had been a hero. Hilda, still sitting at the dining room table, could think of other times her husband had been brave: One time while he was a school psychologist, a troubled kid pulled a knife on him.

— ❄ —

Ray used more than one office in the many schools in which he worked. All of his offices were of a medium size. Many of his offices wore wooden floors. Many people entered into his office daily. Many severely troubled parents, teachers, and, indeed, kids sought guidance. They would talk to him about their troubles, their past, and their frustrations. Some told of their horrifying abuse by close relatives. People shared with the compassionate man their innermost troubles that lurked within their damaged hearts. Ray Beamer was the school psychologist for three counties. Ray Beamer had begun the special education department in several counties. Ray Beamer was admired and respected by nearly all the people with whom he dealt. There were grim exceptions, however....

The day had begun normally; Ray had kissed his wife and kids goodbye, headed to the office, and begun a typical day's work. He sat down in his wooden desk chair and leaned back to look at the daily schedule. On his schedule he saw the name: Billy Loestler. Ray's heart sank.

Billy Loestler was a sick-minded young teenager; a very troubled teenager at that. His entire countenance oozed rebellion. His clothes, his disrespectful attitude, his entire demeanor. Some sort of hatred lurked behind his piercing, evil-reflecting eyes. The boy had been abused almost since birth. The boy had no fear. The boy did not know of God's love. In fact, Ray was the only "Christian" whom he had ever really known. Ray was the only person who had stood up to him; the only person who really put his foot down on Billy. And Billy hated that.

The last time Ray had seen Billy had been before Christmas. Ray gladly imparted the thankfulness and joy of the season's true reason. Billy was coldhearted to the Gospel. Ray had also told him never to swear in his presence again. Billy hated being told what to do.

And so, as Ray held the schedule informing him of his fate, Ray said a silent prayer:

"Lord, I don't know how to handle this kid. I know that You love him unconditionally. Please, help me to stand up to this teenager through Your love, strength, and wisdom. Thank You, Father. In Christ's Name, Amen."

An overall sense of peace, an overall sense of renewed

strength filled his entire being. Little did he know how much he needed that prayer....

It was now after lunch and the day had continued to go on as usual. Neurotic kids. Nervous teachers. Neglectful parents. When Ray walked into his office following his lunch break, he was thinking about his research paper which was to be submitted to the board.

"Hey! Beamer man! What ya gonna tell me to do next?"

At the very second of hearing the voice, Ray's head jerked up in defense and his back straightened up in startled response.

Billy's presence, along with his malice-filled intentions, brought dark tension into the room. Billy's muscular arm grabbed a large chair and, lifting it effortlessly, turned and plopped it onto the floor with a loud thud. With a speedy, slick turn around, he sat on the edge of his chair with his legs far apart. His perch caused him to appear like a lion ready to lunge.

"I don't want to order you around.... Tell me, Billy, how was your Christmas vacation?" Ray tried to divert the attention from rebellion to regeneration. Billy then spit out his reply: "It was fine—why? Why do you care? You just wanna shove me around anyway, man!" After all, Billy wasn't going to tell this "school psychologist" about his Christmas. He'd never impart the truth.... The truth that his dad's new live-in had "stuck a tree up and tossed a stupid gift or two on the floor for her son and didn't give a thing to him" and that the "old man had thrown a beer party for the New Year- with drunks and women hangin' around all over the place." He squinted his dark brown eyes in piercing defiance.

Ray's mind then flew into the quick realization that he might need his prayer far more than he'd even dreamt! This boy in black looked ready to attack anything that Ray said.

The poor boy! He doesn't have a chance without God! He looks so tense, insecure, and sad. His parents are certainly known for crime. Gee, some parents should never be parents! Ray quickly thought.

"Maybe you could tell me more about how your dad's doing."

"No way. You don't care anyway. You're just a fake like all da others."

Ray felt a swell of compassion and love in his heart. Then he began to reply about how sorry he was and how he wanted to help and....

"Ya know what, Beamer? I am sick and tired of puttin' up with people like you!!.... Billy launched and jerked to his full height of six feet. He was now yelling at the loving counselor.

"It's because of....people like you that keep a talkin' and never help!! Where were you when I got so beat til I just didn't care no more? Where were ya when my mom left? Where were ya, huh? WHERE WERE YA?!!"

The possessed acting boy was now completely out of control. He was trembling severely. His eyes reflected the evil with which he spoke.

Ray prayed as he began to notice Billy thrust his shaking arm into his oversized coat which he had continually worn though inside. Out appeared a hunter's knife. He raised it with his clenched fist and slowly, dementedly approached his intended victim.

"Come now, boy! Don't you see? Your dad stopped us. We tried to come. He blocked us...God is loving you right now. He hates the devil that has caused you all of this pain. He hates it so much that He sent His own Son to die for you so that you could escape this life of pain!!!" With every word, with every nearing step of the boy, Ray's voice became louder and louder until the last sentence was cried out in passion for the boy's soul. It wasn't Ray's message. He was too nervous. It was God speaking through Ray to the boy.

All the while, the boy's face seemed to be reflecting an inward revelation. It wasn't the good people's fault! It wasn't the bad people's fault! It was the devil's fault. Billy was becoming like what he hated the most! Suddenly, Billy dropped the knife—and with it all of the hatred. He fell to his knees and sobbed for the first time in years.

"How do you know this God's Son? You seem ta know 'im! Tell me! Tell me!!!" The boy was now crying in a sinner's desperation.

Ray bent down to his level and said, "Don't worry, son. I'll tell you."

He placed a hand on the tear moistened one which had just held the knife, which had just threatened Ray's life!

"Now, son, everybody's a sinner because we've done so many bad things; sins in our lives, and have fallen way short of God. We both know that we deserve to be punished. But God; He's so loving, so forgiving, so merciful! In His great mercy, He sent His Son to receive the punishment in our place. He died on the cross in your place. When He was nailed on the cross, He was thinking of you, Billy. He rose again to conquer the death which we would have suffered. He conquered everything that's bad or evil! John 3:16 is an excellent verse to explain this: 'For God so loved the world, that he gave his only begotten Son that whosoever believeth in him should not perish, but have everlasting life.' And that's the truth, Billy. The Truth with a capital 'T.' In fact, He, at this very moment, wants to come into your heart and be your Savior from all your sins. He wants to live inside of you and love you forever. Do you want this, Billy?"

"Yes, Mr. Beamer! Yes! What do you do to get that stuff?"

"Well, all you have to do is receive the gift and sincerely repent of your sins. All you have to do is just pray the sinner's prayer with all sincerity. Will you do that Billy?"

"Yes! Yes, I will!"

"Okay, pray along right with me. Pray it from your heart, too."

At this, they both bowed their heads with solemn sincerity.

"Dear Jesus, I know that I am a sinner. I also know that You are so good and loving that You died on the cross for me. And I believe it. I confess my sins and ask that you forgive me and wash me from all of it. Please, be my

Savior and Lord. I sincerely repent of my sins. I ask you to please come into my heart and life forever. I believe in You, Jesus. I believe with all of my heart, mind, soul, and strength that You are saving me right now. Thanks so much. In Christ's Name, Amen."

"Boy! I feel like a new guy! Does it last? Do I always get to be saved?" Billy's eyes reflected pure joy and love. He truly was a new creature! His hard, cold face had melted into a loving new boy! Miraculous!

"It'll never leave you, son. You'll be saved no matter what. The entire Bible points to that fact. You will never be the same. You truly are a new creature!" Ray gave the boy a needed hug.

The boy didn't seem to want to let go. Ray got the feeling that he hadn't been hugged for a long, long time. So for a few heartfelt minutes, the boy just clung to Ray. And Ray didn't let go until Billy did. Suddenly, the boy whom he had had a hard time loving, became the student he loved the most. Ray's prayer had been answered beyond his wildest dreams. And so another life was changed (by God) through Ray M. Beamer.

Besides all of the adventurous times in which he had been a brave, heroic figure, Hilda knew something which was much more important to her: He had been there for his family.

Hilda felt better as she closed her diary because she knew that no one could take away the old Ray from her heart. No one.

— ✳ —

Hilda awoke with a start. What had awakened her? Then she heard it again. The doorbell sounded at the oh, so early hour of the morning. Darkness still curtained Le Mars, Iowa. Darkness of despair curtained Hilda.

She rubbed her eyes trying desperately to become alert. She met Ruth in the hall. Ray's bedroom was empty!

Ding ! Dong! The bell sounded again throughout the house adding to their state of panic. Both Hilda and Ruth had thought of his various possible fates. Had Ray been killed by a car while running away? Had he only fallen?

Ruth swung open the front door to stand face to face with a policeman. His car lights beamed in the sleepy street.

"Is Hilda Beamer here?" the policeman inquired. He was tall, middle-aged, and his hair had streaks of gray. In the background, a police radio blared in and out.

"Yes, I'm her daughter," Ruth replied guardedly with adrenaline rushing. Hilda took her place at Ruth's side.

"I'm Hilda," she answered in a trembling, weak voice. Her hands shook violently.

"Well, ma'am, your husband, Ray Beamer, has been taken to the hospital. He's really bruised up and exhausted. He's not pretty."

With an expression of thankfulness, Hilda and Ruth hurried to prepare for the hospital. Again. Another emergency....

Later, having comforted and covered Ray, Hilda regrouped her thoughts. Although many women would have sat down and cried, Hilda sat down and held his hand. He had fallen asleep; the scene was touching yet so very true. Ray's eyes were closed and his mouth open. Hilda's eyes were wearily watching him. Their hands, locked in love, rested on Ray's armrest. No sound imposed except Hilda's soft voice humming a hymn. One of Ray's favorite hymns, "It Is Well With My Soul."

The last wandering of Ray's had almost been too much for Hilda. Details of his running away only left her more panic stricken; if she left Ray unattended, he might reenact his shocking escape! No one had even contemplated what he had performed....

On the night of his escapade, Ray had torn through the back porch window's screen. The tall man with a broad

God granted us this special day. The nursing home took residents fishing; Carrie, Aunt Ruth, and I joined. We didn't catch any fish... But that didn't matter....... Papa and I were together again..... This is our last photo..... In three months, he was gone.....

chest had squeezed through a window no larger than a small suitcase. In darkness, 86 year old Ray dove out head first onto an outdoor chair which had happened to be there. Dropping three feet, Ray received terrible bruises and had been barely able to stand up.

Police found Ray Beamer, the former superintendent of schools, in a sorry state: sitting on a curb, in the chilling night air, clothed in urine soaked pajamas.

The incident went through Hilda's mind innumerable times. She finally faced the sobering fact: Ray could not live at home anymore.

Then the call came; it may have been God's sign for the timing could never have been better. There was an opening in the best Alzheimer's unit in the area. It was time…. It was time.

— ❋ —

"Mary …. I told them I'd place him," Hilda courageously admitted when her elder daughter answered the phone. Her eyes emitted pain and tears.

— ❋ —

August 6, 1999—a date forever etched in Hilda's mind. It was only an ironic few days before their fifty-seventh anniversary. A date that would change the family's lives forever. The day so hard, yet so right.

For some people, the relief would have been celebrated, but for Hilda, it was mourned. For fifty-seven years they had lived together as husband and wife. For over 20,800 days they had shared their lives. Half of her was gone. Half of her would never be the same.

Lisa Niebuhr, a kindhearted social worker and friend from the Alzheimer's Association, gave them support on that difficult day.

The entire atmosphere of the Alzheimer's unit created a soothing environment for the elderly victims. Ray's countenance seemed to show a certain amount of peace which seemed to say, "This is where I belong now. Finally, I don't have to try to fit into your world of noise and confusing people. I'll be just fine."

They were shown his simple, comforting room, went over his daily routines, and kissed him goodbye. Ray and

Hilda Beamer were to live apart for the first time in fifty-seven years. Stoically, tearfully Ruth and she rode home.

But when Hilda stepped onto the carpet in the den, Ray was not there. When Hilda set the table, it was for two, not three. When Hilda went to bed, there was no Ray to kiss goodnight. As Ruth and Hilda glanced at his old recliner, he was not sleeping there. The house was full of reminders of Ruth's dad and Hilda's husband. No Ray; only unshakable memories and unstoppable tears.

EPILOGUE

Just as a beautiful day eventually ends with a sunset, so did a beautiful life. Ray's was a long and at times dramatic one. His sunset is one that he would have hated for he'd been such an intelligent yet kind man. Prior to Alzheimer's, his life was streaked with rejection, happiness, love and faith. He loved his family so much....

Working through her emotions, Mary finally visited her father. With husband and kids in tow, they entered his spacious room. Thankfully, Ray had adjusted remarkably well. God gave them a priceless gift. Ray briefly recognized them. As he hugged his grandkids, he declared beaming in cherished pride,

"You can't beat 'em!" The moment, a flash of light in a diseased dark world, was fleeting but very treasured. He had proudly voiced that statement of affection countless times—before advanced Alzheimer's. Stacie choked back tears—that was her papa.

During their invaluable visit, Ray half-jokingly admitted, "I'm a wonderful guy!" Everyone agreed.

Ruth and Hilda tried to visit Ray every week. Even though the disease destroyed most of their precious moments, one cherished expression of affection remained intact.

More often than not, the nurses would walk past Ray's room and see the touching sight~ Ray and Hilda were still holding hands.

CLOSING STORY

Papa Ray, you were and are a wonderful guy. I love you.
Stacie R. Stoelting —Granddaughter of Ray M. Beamer
November 12, 2000

As I write this, Papa Ray is fighting for life. He is dying. Right now, I'm fighting for him, too. I fight the knowledge of losing another grandparent; in a way, losing Papa to death is like losing him a second time.

Alzheimer's started to steal my papa when I was around two years old. No matter how much it tried, it never stole my memories. Even with Alzheimer's, he was, just like my other grandpa, the best grandpa in the world. Even with Alzheimer's, he was my role model, though not in actions, but in memories.

When I was around four years old, I had a desire to play the piano. He always had loved the piano, too, even though he was never given the chance to learn how to play well. He sat next to me at the old piano in their house and taught me how to play a simple hymn. I know it to this day.

Whenever Christmas arrived, there were toys for Carrie and me. Papa always kept a good, old pocket knife and he'd come to the rescue whenever a toy needed to be released from a box. Papa was a fun friend. When I was a little girl, he would pick me up and play doctor. He always thought that my pretend condition was serious so he would place me on the den sofa and say, "I think we'll have to operate!" He then tickled me to no end! He would play a game with me with his hands. We always had an indescribable bond even though I didn't know the pure Papa very long.

I would listen intently to my family members tell about what a fine man he was, what a fine gentleman. Daddy and he always had a special relationship; he and Papa would watch sports together. With every indication, I'd latch onto any clue that led me to his true personality. He signed his name with his middle initial-Ray M. Beamer; thereafter, whenever I thought of it, I signed my name Stacie R. Stoelting. Papa enjoyed and was good at geometry; thereafter, I took geometry. Papa loved bread and butter. I love bread and butter. Papa was a strong man. I try to be strong, too. He loved the hymn, "It Is Well With My Soul." I played it almost continuously on the piano. He had a special walk. I tried to do the Papa Ray walk when I was little. (Only when I was older did I realize that he walked that way not out of confidence but because of polio.)

Papa and I stuck up for one another. If we were at a larger family gathering and one of us wanted to talk, the other person would be sure that the other was heard.

Papa and I shared a lot in common. Papa enjoyed a good joke, had a quick wit, loved our family infinitely, and my, how he loved hymns! (Even with Alzheimer's, he'd still sing the good old hymns with not so much as a missed note.) He was a good husband, father, father in law, grandpa, neighbor, and friend. He'd stand up for you if you were down. His smile lit up a crowd. His kindness won him many friends. His unconditional love encompassed all of his family. You felt that love in his presence. When Papa was still home, still suffering from Alzheimer's, Grandma and he would hold hands, kiss, and tell of their great love for one another. He always said, "You're a good woman." To which Grandma would similarly reply: "You're a good husband, honey." Their love never ended. After all, perfect love is from God and God is love.

Yes, I wrote a book about their love-filled lives and their battle with Alzheimer's. It was the least I could do. Their outstanding, God-honoring lives required some sort of record. The treasure, the legacy needed to be preserved.

Papa would be happy about the legacy he's leaving behind. All of his descendants are born again believers. Carrie and I are the next generation to carry on the Gift. Believe me, we'll try to make him proud.

Note: Painfully, I type: Papa Ray M. Beamer, my hero, died a few hours after I wrote this. It comforts me to think: In Heaven, he's still loving us now as we are loving him still.

MEMORIES

Papa Ray's Obituary

Ray M. Beamer

Ray M. Beamer, age 87, of Le Mars, died Sunday, November 12, 2000 at Floyd Valley Memorial Hospital in Le Mars, Iowa. Services will be held at the Le Mars Bible Church at 10:00 AM, Thursday, November 16, 2000, with Pastor Ken Koth and Pastor Fred Gums officiating. Visitation will be Wednesday, November 15, 2000 beginning at 2:00 PM. and the family prayer service at 7:00 PM. Burial will be at the Tecumseh Cemetery in Tecumseh, Nebraska.

Ray Beamer was born December 17, 1912 in DuBois, Nebraska the son of Bernice and Nellie (Keeler) Beamer. Mr. Beamer graduated from the Pawnee City High School in 1931. He received his bachelor of science degree at Peru State Teachers College, and later received a masters degree from the University of Nebraska where he met and later married Hilda Hazen. They were married August 9, 1942 in Tecumseh, Nebraska. Mr. Beamer took extensive graduate work at the University of Iowa and the University of Colorado.

Ray Beamer dedicated his life to children; their well-being and education. He taught in the rural schools of Nebraska City, Pawnee City, and Tecumseh, Nebraska (where he also farmed). He served as a principal and later as superintendent at Syracuse, Nebraska. He taught and coached at Murray, Iowa and Deloit, Iowa. He directed special education classes and coached in Denision, Iowa.

He served developmentally disabled children by establishing classes for them as a supervisor for Plymouth County's disabled children and their families. He was the director of special education for both Sioux and Plymouth counties until his retirement in 1977. Mr. Beamer's dedication to children was extensive. He wanted every child to reach his potential and encouraged them to reach their best educational level possible. He wanted them to feel loved and appreciated because then, and only then, could they reach their potential. Ray spent his career testing and counseling children along with their parents and teachers. He wanted parents and teachers to work as a team for the child's benefit.

As a young man, Mr. Beamer was a member of the Presbyterian Church in Pawnee City, Nebraska where he accepted Christ as a young boy. In later years he was a member of Le Mars Bible Church in Le Mars, Iowa. He was a member of Phi Delta Kappa. He was a past member also of the Lions Club. He was a wonderful and loving husband, father, father-in-law and grandpa.

Survivors include his wife Hilda of Le Mars, two daughters Ruth Beamer of Le Mars and Mary Stoelting and her husband Dr. Wendell Stoelting, and his two beloved granddaughters Stacie Ruth and Carrie Beth of Cherokee. His sister Mildred Dry and her husband Paul, of Bella Vista, Arkansas and several nieces, nephew and cousins. Two nieces Dorothy and Lowell Perry of Des Moines, Iowa, Margaret and her husband Bud Ripperger of Creston, Iowa, a nephew Dr. Richard Reel of West Des Moines, a niece Barbara Betz and her husband Stuart of Rogers, Arkansas, and several great nieces and cousins. He also leaves behind his dear friends and neighbors of 38 years, Mert and Katy Den Hartog.

He was preceded in death by his parents and his sister Alice Charter.

November 13, 2000

Dearest Daddy,

Last night you met Jesus. How wonderful, for you,
Daddy! We've had a great time of fellowship with both
Pastor Ken, Pastor Fred, and Kami. They've taken such
good care of us. Stacie asked Pastor Fred whether or not
you can continue to think about us from Heaven. She
said that she knows that while we're loving you, you're
still loving us. Well, Daddy, if by chance you can know
what's happening here, we know that it's with delight
that you are using your new alert mind and a body now
working so beautifully. So here's a little thank you letter
and a tribute to you, our precious daddy.

People will have read about your dedication to
children's education, and we of course are proud of that-
but what really counted to both of us was your dedication to your family and your unconditional love. Each of
us always felt that love and support and we could always count on you.

Although we're both middle aged women now, we
cling to our memories of your strong hugs and the way
you held our hands. Never, under any circumstance, did
you withdraw your love or show any favoritism. We are
opposites, you know, yet we each always felt so special.

Thanks for being such a romantic husband to Mama. Always we observed the love and the romance which you two shared. That love paid off for you, Daddy, when Alzheimer's robbed you of your many abilities. Mama, as you may know, was so kind and patient. You continued to hold hands and tell each other that you loved one another in spite of Alzheimer's disease. Little did you know that your granddaughter, Stacie, would write a book about your life and your relationship with Mama. Carrie Beth intends to research your family's history and she wishes with all her heart that she could have remembered you prior to the onset of Alzheimer's. Both girls love to hear how you love them.

The Lord knew which daughter was to remain single for a time. Your Ruthie was so dedicated to you, Daddy. She treated you with such love and provided you with every possible stimulating activity. She cherished you as a person not as a <u>victim</u> of the disease. I believe that you knew that Ruthie was always there for you. Somehow, about now, I can see you rolling your blue eyes, shrugging your shoulders, and saying in jest, "I must have done something right!"

You did, Daddy. Along with an example of a great marriage and a stable home, you imparted your faith in such a way that when we individually accepted Jesus as our Savior, it was quite easy to accept the concept of our Heavenly Father's love. Thank you so much, Daddy.

We rejoice that you're experiencing His joy, His presence, His love. We are experiencing God's Holy Spirit and we have such comfort and peace. We're going to miss you, Daddy, but because of your legacy of faith, love, and laughter—we're going to be just fine.

All of our love,
Your girls

WELCOME TO MY HAPPY CHILDHOOD "PAPA RAY" MEMORIES ....

In the next few pages, you are invited to go back in time where you can see the true Papa I loved and continued to love. These are only a few of the many cherished memories I possess.

King of the Air

Flying through a castle of many clouds, an eagle sails unheard.
Strong, sure wings adorn the enormous, graceful bird.

As though acting like a royal king,
It glides through the obeying air.
It dips upward and glides downward—fancy at wing;
Making heads turn in an astonishing stare.

It beats its wings dramatically as it soars to a new altitude.
Glittering eyes show its powerful will.
Its head, held high, shows its confident attitude;
Then it glides to its nest and sits quite still.

God made eagles as He did you and me.
God is the Highest Majesty!

By Stacie Ruth Stoelting
AGE 11

NOTE: I shared this with Papa; little did I know that within a few years, he wouldn't be able to understand it.

Papa and I enjoyed laughing together! Here, my mother said he teased me and we were laughing once again. I still <u>love</u> to laugh.

Papa Ray, Grandma Hilda, Carrie and I enjoyed dancing together. It was such fun! Here we are doing a funny dance move. So—what do you think? Are we good dancers?!

GOD LOVES YOU, I KNOW

*This a song which I composed
for my beloved Papa Ray in his honor:*

*First Verse:
God loves you, I know, And He'll take care of you, I know.
But it's hard sometimes, to understand,
How this is right in God's own hands.
So I say goodbye in sad dismay,
But I will remember happier days,
For I know, I'll see you some day....*

*Second Verse:
When this life on earth, is full of tears
And our minds reflect on more happy years,
I will remember God and His grace;
So now smiling with Christ I see your face,
And praising Him, I hear your voice,
Yes, it brings me joy
For I'll see you some day....*

*Refrain:
I'll see you in Heaven! Where we will be most free
to worship Christ together,
And live in love eternally.
Yes, I know....*

*Last Refrain:
I'll see you in Heaven!
Where we will be most free
To worship Christ together,
And live in love eternally.
Yes, I know....
God loves you!*

*Dedicated to you, Papa Ray.
Love in Christ, Stacie, Age 16*

Somehow, Papa's lap was one of the comfiest! We would snuggle during movies or if I began to tire—(with me, tiring was rare!)

By this picture, you can certainly see that Papa was a tolerant man! We're attempting to do his hair. (I stress <u>attempt</u>.) Those were such happy days....

"Happy Eleventh Birthday Stacie!" Papa Ray and Grandma rolled out a brand-new, beautiful bike! (I have it to this day!)

Grandma Hilda (holding me at age three) and Papa Ray (holding my baby sister Carrie) were wonderful babysitters! We loved it!

A dance lesson— Papa Style!

Carrie, Papa, Daddy, and me. We were quite a team! We were pals!

WHEN PAPA & I WENT TO PLAY

by Stacie R. Stoelting

Oh! It was a special day!
When Papa and I went to play.
The sun was high
Our joy was nigh
When Papa and I
Went to play.

"Oh, Papa! Papa! Can we swing?"
I, the child, jumped like a spring!
"Sure! Let's go right now!"
Papa said with a smile
He nodded in his style.
And we stepped awhile.
We went to play.

Papa lifted me up onto the seat
And as a very special treat-
He joined me on the swing for two.
And I truly, surely knew
That there were few papas who
Would swing, too.
And so we played.

"Higher! Higher!" I would squeal.
"Are you sure?" Papa appealed.
"Oh, yes!" I said. As soon as my reply
We rushed through air and touched the sky!
At least we did in a child's eye.
At least we did try and I did cry:
"Oh, Papa! It's so much fun to play!"

Someday, in Heaven, I will say:
"Oh, Papa! Let us go to play!"
"Why, sure!" He will reply.
And so we'll swing so very high.
And that time we'll truly touch the sky.
We both will be there to stay.
Then nothing will stop our play.......

Oh, yes ... This is <u>the swingset</u>! Papa and I loved to play there! This was the first time I'd ever played on it.

Oh, it was a special day! Papa and I went to play on my first, brand new swing-set! I was only about three years old but I still remember it. When I saw the swing and the slide I joyously said: "I'm so happy!!" I hope you enjoyed my heartfelt poem...

These are my precious papas. Papa Otto and Papa Ray always got along well. Papa Otto is in his nineties here and Papa Ray is in his eighties. I loved and love them so much. They are probably together quite often in their Heavenly mansions! (This picture was taken at my eleventh birthday party. We always had birthday parties with them.)

CHRISTMAS AND PAPAS

Working through grief, I wrote this Christmas Memory dedicated to both of my papas. May this bless their memories always:

Christmas and Grandpas, for me, go together. Every fond Yuletide memory has been sagaciously spent with my papas; always, they knew how to make a beautiful holiday even better. Whether it was their greeting grins at the door on Christmas morning or a nap on their laps on Christmas afternoon, they were forever faithful (with classic twinkles in their eyes) to make my Christmas uniquely special.

Papa Ray's and Papa Otto's treasured homes were dazzling to me as a very young child. Their ancient Christmas trees were laden with lights and they illuminated the rooms with their sparkling rainbows. The Christ-centered, porcelain Nativity eloquently stood as a representative of the true celebration. Both warm abodes overflowed with the scents of Christmas itself. Grandmas' Christmas goodies pleasantly permeated the air.

Both papas had not only a good taste in food, they also had fine taste in choosing their wives. Mutually, the number of years spent with my precious grandmas totaled 112 years! Both grandmas continue to be culinary queens; neither grandpa had to fret about food. Maybe that's why Papa Otto could sacrifice the bank's fruit cake for the granddaughters. Yet tasty delicacies were not the only integral part of the happy holiday—presents were, too!

Presents piled high under the tree; the granddaughters anxiously awaited the toys! Papa Ray's trusty old pocket knife always rescued the entrapped toys from binding packages to his granddaughters' squealing delight. Papa Otto delighted in displaying his Santa Claus which merrily played Christmas carols; from this, the pleased grandpa would receive laughing little girls.

Yes, Christmas and Grandpas go together. But this Christmas won't be the same. Seven months ago, Papa Otto passed away; this week Papa Ray left me, too. I'm sixteen now, but celebrating Christmas without my heroes will be terribly hard. This year, my papas left me to celebrate Christmas in Heaven. The pocket knife, the musical Santa Claus are both put away....

Christmas and Grandpas . . . Is there any batter way to celebrate Christmas? We were enthusiastically celebrating and were all smiles! I was overjoyed —after all, my grandparents were there! (Do you like my Christmas dress?)

Here we are at my Stoelting grandparents' home. (Papa Ray and Grandma Hilda drove all the way over) Papa always came to the rescue if I couldn't open my present! By the looks on our faces, one would think it's a serious procedure!

It's Christmas and Papa let us have extra special candy! You can tell that I was overjoyed to have chocolate—I'm still a chocolate fan!

Ray & Hilda holding hands at their fifty-fourth anniversary........ Papa Ray was in the middle stage of the disease.

Left to right. Carrie, Mama, (me) and Grandma Hilda. Here, we are having a traditional birthday blast! We were celebrating Mom's birthday. (Don't worry, Mom, I won't tell what age!)

AFTERWORD

John 14:12 - Verily, verily, I say unto you, He that believeth on me, the works that I do shall he do also; and greater works than these shall he do; because I go unto my Father.

And so, this was Ray and Hilda's story. A story of love. A story of triumph over adversity. A story to help others. If you are suffering through a similar situation with a loved one, please, contact the Alzheimer's Association. Don't hesitate. Don't worry. They are there to help—not to manipulate and invade your privacy. May this story lead you to contact this wonderful organization.

Their's truly was a story of faith. Nothing in the world helped Grandma Hilda except her faith. She, as well as our family, received Christ as Savior. Do you know Him as your personal Savior? May I invite you to become a child of God. I'm not writing about a religion, I'm writing about a <u>personal relationship</u> with the living, loving God. He is my Best Friend. He is real. He is true. Please, read this excerpt copied from Billy Graham's website:

How To Become A Christian:
The central theme of the Bible is God's love for you and for all people. This love was revealed when Jesus Christ, the Son of God, came into the world as a human being, lived a sinless life, died on the cross, and rose from the dead. Because Christ died, your sins can be forgiven, and because He conquered death you can have eternal life. You can know for sure what will become of you after you die. You have probably heard the story of God's love referred to as the "Gospel." The word Gospel simply means "Good News." The Gospel is the Good

News that, because of what Christ has done, we can be forgiven and can live forever.

But this gift of forgiveness and eternal life cannot be yours unless you willingly accept it. God requires an individual response from you. The following verses from the Bible show God's part and yours in this process:

God's love is revealed in the Bible. "For God so loved the world that he gave his one and only Son, that whoever believes in him shall not perish but have eternal life" (John 3:16). God loves you. He wants to bless your life and make it full and complete. And He wants to give you a life which will last forever, even after you experience physical death.

We are sinful. "For all have sinned and fall short of the glory of God" (Romans 3:23). You may have heard someone say, "I'm only human—nobody's perfect." This Bible verse says the same thing: We are all sinners. We all do things that we know are wrong. And that's why we feel estranged from God—because God is holy and good, and we are not.

Sin has a penalty. "For the wages of sin is death" (Romans 6:23). Just as criminals must pay the penalty for their crimes, sinners must pay the penalty for their sins. If you continue to sin, you will pay the penalty of spiritual death: You will not only die physically; you will also be separated from our holy God for all eternity. The Bible teaches that those who choose to remain separated from God will spend eternity in a place called hell.

Christ has paid our penalty. "But God demonstrates his own love for us in this: While we were still sinners, Christ died for us" (Romans 5:8). The Bible teaches that Jesus Christ, the sinless Son of God, has paid the penalty for all your sins. You may think you have to lead a good life and do good deeds before God will love you. But the Bible says that Christ loved you enough to die for you, even when you were rebelling against Him.

Salvation is a free gift. "For it is by grace you have been saved, through faith—and this not from yourselves, it is the gift of God—not by works, so that no one can boast" (Ephesians 2:8-9). The word grace means "undeserved favor." It means God is offering you something you could never provide for yourself: forgiveness of sins and eternal life, God's gift to you is free. You do not have to work for a gift. All you have to do is joyfully receive it. Believe with all your heart that Jesus Christ died for you!

Christ is at your heart's door. "Here I am! I stand at the door and knock. If anyone hears my voice and opens the door, I will come in and eat with him, and he with me" (Revelation 3:20). Jesus Christ wants to have a personal relationship with you. Picture, if you will, Jesus Christ standing at the door of your heart (the door of your emotions, intellect and will). Invite Him in; He is waiting for you to receive Him into your heart and life.

You must receive Him. "Yet to all who received him, to those who believed in his name, he gave the right to become children of God" (John 1:12). When you receive Christ into your heart you become a child of God, and have the privilege of talking to Him in prayer at any time about anything. The Christian life is a personal relationship to God through Jesus Christ. And best of all, it is a relationship that will last for all eternity.

Yes, this is me. This picture was taken at a Christian party shortly before the hardest seven months of my life. Within mere months, both of my papas were in Heaven. (Age fifteen.)

Words aren't necessary......

Use this Coupon to Order Additional Copies of Still Holding Hands

Please ship *Still Holding Hands* to:

Name _____ Address _____

City _____ State _____ Zip _____

Phone Number_____ Fax Number _____

		Quantity	Total
Orders shipped via Air Mail the day they are received.	Still Holding Hands	$14.95 each	$ _____
	Shipping and Handling 3.00 each No S and H with purchase of two books or more.		$ _____
		Grand Total	$ _____

Credit Card Number _____ ❏ VISA

Expiration Date _____ Signature _____ ❏ MasterCard

Publication Consultants

PO Box 221974
Anchorage, AK 99518
Phone (907) 349-1424 • Fax (907) 349-1426
www.alaskabooks.biz •email: books@alaskabooks.biz

VISA **MasterCard**

To schedule book signings and reserve
guest appearances, kindly contact:

Stacie Stoelting
930 Hillside St.
P.O. Box 558
Cherokee, IA, 51012

Or phone reservations at (712) 225-2161.